Sleepy Willie
Sings the Blues

4496-MUNG

Sleepy Willie Sings the Blues

Horace Mungin

To order additional copies of this book, contact:
Xlibris Corporation
1-888-7-XLIBRIS
www.Xlibris.com
Orders@Xlibris.com

Contents

VAUGHN, KEVIN, MALCOLM,
SHARNECE,
RASHIDA,LATEEF,
KAMILAH, AKIL
THE NEXT GENERATION.

IN MEMORY OF WILLIAM (SLEEPY WILLIE) WALKER

INTRODUCTION

I grew up in a mid-Manhattan neighborhood that borders Hell's Kitchen. My neighborhood got its name from the many battles between the African Americans who lived down the hill towards Eleventh Avenue, and the whites that lived on top of the hill on Amsterdam Avenue. These battles took place while the memory of Teddy Roosevelt's famous charge up San Juan Hill in Cuba, during the Spanish/American War, was still fresh in people's minds. Thus, through comparison, the area between 60th street and 64th street, Amsterdam Avenue to Eleventh Avenue became known as San Juan Hill.

When my Family moved there from Harlem, in 1950, the area had been re-named after the Amsterdam Housing Projects built in 1947. But many old timers still called the area San Juan Hill. Among these old timers was a man named William Walker. I was first introduced to Mr. William (Sleepy Willie) Walker, who was nearly thirty years my senior, in 1963, by some mutual friends. I was twenty-one and had just returned to the neighborhood from a sprint in the army. The Amsterdam Community was unique in several ways, but one particular way gave it a refreshing vigor. There were no age barriers in the community's unspoken code of conduct. On the weekends groups of men of all ages hung out on the benches that lined the basketball court in the park on 64th street, watching the play, listening to music or baseball games, and, of course, talking jive.

The predominant speaker was always Sleepy Willie, who performed masterful recitals of street lore and brilliant portrayals of the shoddy events of ivory tower elitist. I can't be certain how William Walker came by the nickname "Sleepy Willie." I will speculate that it may have been because he had huge bags under his eyes and his eyelids drooped, making him appear asleep. But when it got down to social awareness, Sleepy Willie never slept. Willie kept his listeners spellbound with his engaging interpretations of the occurrences of everyone from street thugs to presidents (he had a field day with Richard Nixon and O.J. Simpson). Willie viewed everything from the most unorthodox angles, like a musician who plays an unexpected note, which makes the listener reappraise his previous judgement. Willie's narratives were replete with whimsical flare and eccentric spins that went so far out there that they nearly always surprised everyone by concluding within the realm of reasonableness. That man could tell a story.

Over the years Willie and I became good personal friends despite our age different, but in truth, Willie was friend to everyone in our community. I always studied Willie's storytelling style closely. What he did was really meaningful to me, although, at the time, I was unaware that I would one day adapt it to my own use. I'm today brash enough to think that I learned more from Willie's storytelling then any other in his audience. In later years I analyzed his technique and incorporated it into a fictional character by the same name.

In 1963 I got married and move to the Bronx, but I always returned to my old stomping grounds to visit my mother (who stills lives there today), and the old gang. I always found Willie reigning supreme. And so it went for another thirty years. In the late 70's I wrote a weekly syndicated newspaper column. In the column I satirized political and social topics, often featuring a developing character named Sleepy Willie. The column had a six-year run and in 1991 a collection of the columns were published under the title "Sleepy Willie Talks About Life."

The sketches in the first book were terse seven hundred word pieces because of the space limitation of a newspaper column. Also, the topics were contemporary events of the week with points that had to be reached quickly. A weekly newspaper column has to confer the sense of immediacy.

The current book takes the long view. The sketches presented here are a lengthier discourse of Willie unique way of circling a subject's peripheral elements and weaving it all to a grand finale. Plus, the themes are broader and, for the most part, non-derivative of any specific current event. All the sketches were written with this book in mind save one. "Congressmen and Suitcases" is a column written in the late seventies and it also appeared in the previous book. Because the topic remains so applicable to the real problem of political fund raising I felt it appropriate to re-introduce it here.

I've stated that the sketches in this book are not direct products of specific current events, but, of course, the forty-one shots in a vestibule in the Bronx put words in Willie's mouth. The racist ranting of conservative talk radio hosts put words into Willie's mouth. The misdirected action of many young people put words in Willie's mouth. The scandal prone leaders in Washington, D.C. put words in Willie's mouth. The decline of civility on television put words in Willie's mouth. The teacher who wrote on a child's face put words in Willie's mouth. The young gay man beaten, tired, and left to die, put words in Willie's mouth. All of these events and others make Sleepy Willie sing the blues.

4496-MUNG

LETTER FROM SOUTH

"**E**caroh Lee, my man, I might have to go back South one of these days," Sleepy Willie said.

"Man, you haven't been back in the South since you left in 1933. What makes you think that you'll return now?" I asked.

"The letters I received from Sara Ann Walker, my brother Charles' oldest child. Sara lived with me for four years while she attended college here in the city."

"You had a niece here and I never met her?"

"Ecaroh, you're my man, but I never have my family mingle with people I know from the streets."

"Oh, I see," I said trying to let Willie know that he had hurt my feelings, "your family is too good for me huh?"

"This was a little before we started our weekly meeting," Willie said without apology. When she got her degree, she fled the city saying New York City wasn't a fit place to live in. She even tried to persuade me to go back to South Carolina with her. I tried to persuade her to start her working life here in the city where there are far more opportunities. That battle turned out to be a draw. Sara went back home and has done pretty well for herself. And, as you know, I stayed in the South Bronx, but she still writes letters inviting me back home to South Carolina. Listen to one of her early letters."

> *Dear Uncle Willie:*
>
> *I hope you are well. We are all okay here except for Daddy,*

which is the reason for my letter. I will get to that in a moment. It has been a long time since we've heard from you, or even about you. It almost seems you've given us up as family. I hope this isn't true because we all love you and want so badly to see you. Daddy hasn't seen you since he and Mommy came to New York for my graduation all those many years ago.

Mommy told me that it was a waste of my time trying to get you to come home to South Carolina. She says that you enjoy being isolated from the family. Mommy says, any man who wouldn't attend his own brother's funeral just because it was in the South wouldn't come South to visit his last brother sick in the hospital. This made me feel ambiguous about your not ever visiting. I was happy that it wasn't something you held against the family that prevents you from coming home, but rather, something you hold against the South. You know I feel I can work on that.

Uncle Willie, the South and certainly South Carolina, isn't the way it was when you left. Today we live in the New South. Sure there is still room for improvements, but you won't find any more racism in the South today than you have in New York. The only way I can prove this to you is for you to come see for yourself. There is no better time then now. Your only living brother is in the hospital and wants to see you. I know, from the time I spent with you, that you are a good man. I know that you really love your family. I remember all the questions you asked me about the family when I lived with you. I think you miss being in our lives.

Uncle Willie, we love you and want to see you.

I hope to hear from you soon.

Love and kisses

Sleepy Willie Sings the Blues

Sara Walker

P.S. Uncle Willie, Precisely what is it that you have against
the South?

"Hey that's bad news Willie. You mean to tell me that you didn't
attend your brother's funeral. Man that's cold," I said.

"That was ten years ago," Willie said, "and it was a hard
decision, but I once made a pledge I had to remain true too."

"What about your brother in the hospital, are you going to
see him? Family has got to stick together. You would be the first
person to say that Willie."

"My brother Charles has been out of the hospital for three
months now—he's even gone back to work. I talked with him on
the telephone, he's just fine."

"Well did you at least answer your niece's letter?"

" I did. I wanted to explain to her why I hadn't been back to
the South since I left in thirty-three. Here's my letter."

My dearest Niece Sara:
I received your letter and I'm proud that you think about
your old uncle once in a while. I'm also glad that all of
you in South Carolina are doing good—for that I thank
our Heavenly Host. Say hello to your mama for me. She is
my favorite.

Sara, honey, I'm going to tell you why I have not
been back past the Mason/Dixon since I first escape South
Carolina. I was so grateful to get out of that hellhole that
I made a solemn oath that I would never again set foot on
Southern soil—not even in death.

The New South? That may be, but I'm the same old
Willie. The history of my youth in the South isn't new or
changed. The history of my youth is the history of the old
South and that history is chiseled into my very soul. You
see the South took something from me that it can't give

back. I will never forget or forgive the South for what it did to my people, me, and itself. Yes—itself, you see you can't deprive a people without diminishing yourself. The black race was held in degradation by a degenerate white race. And we were both diminished by it.

From the moment of my birth until the day I got out of the South, my life was controlled, impeded, and violated. Why those crackers were so locked in a mentality that was so insecure that it created "Whites Only" water fountains to give the illusion of race superiority. My youth was spent under the lash and it wasn't until I fled North that I experienced a degree of human dignity.

The New South? The only South I know is the one I fled from many years ago. A place where the black man was burdened with the full weight of oppression, hopelessness, and the white man's boorish treatment. This was a place where a black man's life wasn't worth a wisp of wind. The history of the South is littered with trees that bear strange fruit with blood at its root and terror everywhere. A famous lady sung about it. It was this South that made me do something I can't talk about here. Something only God may understand.

Sara, until the New South can give me back the hope and promise of my youth; make me sixteen again and give me opportunity and dignity on the soil of my birth, I don't want to see it. I know this all sounds born of bitterness, but it's an irreversible situation.

I pray my brother will recover and be home to his family soon. I know he understands my absence. I hope you will—sooner or later. I love you all.

Peace,

Uncle Willie Walker

"Man, that sounds so final," I'd said. "I guess you haven't heard from your niece after that."

"Several times," Willie said. "As a matter of fact, she wrote to me the day her father came home from the hospital. From the tone of her letter, I feel she understands my position better, although she didn't say so. She did say that she thinks I ought to forget and forgive, but to me that would be the same as the Jews forgetting the holocaust. Something that ain't about to happen—not in ten thousand years."

"The Jews may not forget or forgive," I said, "but Jews go to Germany."

"Yeah, but they go to Germany to make sure the Germans don't forget."

"Well," I said, "isn't that worth the trip?"

"Ummm." Willie hummed.

4496-MUNG

SOUTHERN BORN

Sleepy Willie is different. I don't think I shall ever know another person like him. William (Sleepy Willie) Walker is, simultaneously, simple and complex. He is mostly, a self-educated, world observer with opinions on everything there is to ponder. It is his political and social ideology that sets him apart. His thinking reveals a kind of systematic chaos that somehow reaches reasonable conclusions. He views the events of the world through lenses all his own. In Willie's world, politicians would govern without corruption. Hospitals would treat all the sick. Policemen would police honorably. Students would learn eagerly. Workers would all earn a living wage. Poverty would be eliminated. There would be one subway World Series each decade, and the South would apologize for the conditions he fled many years ago. All of these are very desirable things. It is, however, the unorthodoxy of his thinking process that accentuates Willie from others. Reasonable people know that, as desirable as these things are, they are impossible to achieve perfectly, so reasonable people measure their satisfaction with the state of these conditions in degrees. Sleepy Willie uses a different yardstick.

William Walker was the first person I met when I moved to the Bronx many years ago. I was in the Two Cousins bar waiting for my cousin Nate who was late. Nate frequented the bar and knew the people. He had invited me for a drink to welcome me to my new neighborhood and to introduce me around. I drank a beer while I waited. The old man sat at the first table near the window with a view of the street. He wore a gray suit with a blue plaid shirt and a red tie. His face was pleasant; his skin was smooth and caramel color. His gray hair contrasted nicely with his complexion. He had bags the size of a quarter under his eyes. His brown fedora hat was in the empty chair next to him. He overheard me asking the barmaid if she knew Nate and had she seen him this evening. The old man invited me to his table. He introduced himself and we struck up a conversation. He told me that he knew Nate and that Nate usually showed up around this time. I found out that we were both from South Carolina, he from Beaufort, and I from Hollywood. I ordered myself another beer and asked Willie if he wanted one. He accepted. Thus began what, over twenty years, has resulted in a costly, one-sided, but satisfying relationship. A relationship that has been, for me, both educational and entertaining. Over the many years of this friendship, we have discussed anything and everything. War, politics, racism, greed, love, music, the South, poverty, Wall Street, marriage, riots, police brutality, civil rights, art, food, sports, literature, religion, and who is going to pay for the beers, has been our running themes for over two decades now.

"Willie," I asked him one night at the Two Cousins bar, why are you so contrary?"

"Because I was born Southern." He said.

"That just doesn't answer it for me," I said.

"Because I was born a Negro in the South during the time of great darkness."

"Well, if you insist on changing the subject from you to the South, then tell me something about the South you have avoided talking about ever since we first met."

"There is nothing I won't talk about—that is—if I know something about it. What is it you want to know?"

"Why did you leave South Carolina?"

"That was many years ago." Willie's face turned solemn. His

eyes sadden as an amazing transformation took place that told me that this time he was going to talk about *it*. I had no idea what the *it* would be, only that the time had come for details that had, until this moment, been painted over with a broad brush. "A long time ago," Willie lamented.

"What was it that made you have to leave South Carolina?"

"I was born," Willie said, "in Beaufort Country, in an area on the Coosaw River. There were six children, Mama and Daddy. We were three boys and three girls. I was the third oldest child. We lived off the river and the land. Daddy had a fish stand under a moss-tree by the road outside of town. We sold fish, and shrimp, year around, and conch, and oyster in season. Daddy had two string-woven throw nets and a small wooden boat. He and George, the oldest boy, went out at night to catch fish and shrimp. He got ice from the icehouse and sold his goods at the stand, out of a number ten tin wash tub. We had a one-room schoolhouse two miles from our house towards Beaufort. After school, most days, me and my younger brother went to the stand to relieve George. The girls went home to help Mama around the house and in the garden. George would go home to eat, and help Daddy in the fields. In the evening George came back with the horse and wagon to take us and the wash tub home. Daddy and George generally went to bed early to get up at mid-night to go in the river."

"Look, Willie, if you don't want to rehash this—forget it man, I feel like I'm prying."

"I don't need any sympathy from you," Willie said. "The can is open now, let the worms crawl out. Anyway, this was mostly our routine. This was an area of dirt poor blacks and poor whites. This was a time when poor whites had one big advantage over poor blacks—the promotion and protection of the system. The county system, the state system, the federal system, and the custom of the South, worked in the favor of poor whites over any class of black. I'm talking about subjugation. This was a time when even the most educated and prosperous black person in the state had to knuckle under to any white person no matter what their station. You know about this period in American history."

"Yes." I nodded.

"There was three white brothers each with two sons. Two of the brothers owned a general store and were relatively well off. They lived with their families in town. The other brother was a farmer and didn't seem to do so well. His family lived out in the country like us. They had a farm about half way between our one-room schoolhouse and Beaufort. I can't remember many times when all six of those cousins weren't together. The ones that lived in town spent most of their time out at the farm. They were all older than I was. A few of them were even older than my brother George. Their fathers were known as the most brutal racist in the county. They cheated black people, treated them mean, and were often violent with them. The fruit don't fall far from the tree.

"The three sets of cousins learned from their fathers how black people should be treated. All of the young black children in the area had to be aware of them, but because of our proximity they got to practice their racist apprenticeship most often on my brothers and me. I spent all my young life in fear of those thugs. They ambushed us at every point. On Saturdays after our chores we walked to town to buy sweets and pal around, but if we ran into them, they'd chase us down the road with rocks and foul words. Sometimes they would hide in the woods by the road from our schoolhouse and pelt us with rocks and tree branches. One day while me and my younger brother were working at the fish stand, two of them called us away with the promise of a piece of candy. We didn't believe them, but we thought it would be less trouble if we went to them. While we were gone, the other four pissed in the tub of fish. They all ran off laughing and congratulating each other. My brother and I cried.

"Terrorist, that's what they were. Young terrorist learning the tradition of keeping the Negro in their place the Southern way, through fear and intimidation. There were never any response to any of the protest and pleads to the parents of the terrorist. In fact, it seemed the incidence intensified after someone went to the parents with a complaint. These young ruffians had the whole black community frightened that one of these incidences would escalate to a great catastrophe. That's what everybody said.'One day something's gonna happen.' Well something did happen years later.

"I was sixteen years old. One day I took some tools to the ironworks to leave for sharpening. I was walking home from town by myself. It was too late to duck when I saw the six of them on the road, so I continued to walk straight ahead. It had been a long while since I had any trouble with them. I said a silent prayer that this would be a trouble-free encounter. When we met up, they formed a circle around me and started pushing me into one or another of them. They were taunting me and whooping it up like cowboys on a round up. I don't know what caused it, but I lost all fear and the next time they pushed me into one, I lit into him with everything I had. I lowered my head and gave him a butt that drew blood before he hit the ground. I jumped on him and started to beat him with my fist, but the others piled on me pushing my face close to the one on the ground. They were hitting me and trying to pull me up. I grabbed the ear of the one beneath me between my teeth. When they pulled me up I still had a good piece of it in my mouth. They start out to beat me pretty good, but the wounded one hollered with such horror that they stopped to take him to the town's doctor. I laid on the ground not far from the severed piece of ear.

I knew that this was it that I would have to leave town. I couldn't go home because I didn't want to make more trouble for my family. I figured that if I were missing, when those boys made their accusation, my family and others would think that they had killed me. I mean what is the likelihood that I could have bitten off the ear of one of them and survived? Even the white people would have, at least for a while, assumed me dead. I could use the time it took them to figure out what happened to make my escape. I traveled through the night to my uncle's house. I arrived at daybreak and woke the whole family with loud stumbling. I could tell from their eyes that I had been beaten worse than I knew. I told them what had happened and they agreed that there should be no contact with my family. I stayed in bed for a week recovering from my whipping. During this time my uncle made arrangements to get me to Charleston where he had purchased a ticket for me on a boat to New York City. He had contacted his oldest daughter who lived there to put me in her custody."

"A boat?" I said, somewhat surprised.

"Yes, a boat. So there you have it. How I left South Carolina, and why I left South Carolina. On the way up To New York City I swore before God that I would never return to the South. When my cousin picked me up at the fourteen street piers, the first thing I asked her to do was to take me to a church where I made a solemn oath that me and the South was through."

"Was it long before your family knew that you were safe?"

"No, my uncle told my family that I was staying in San Juan Hill, New York City, with Cousin Vera Mae Walker. And it wasn't long before Daddy moved the family to an area in Charleston County. From then on we kept in touch by mail."

"And you've never been back?"

"Never."

"But what about when your folks passed?"

"Now you have touch something I don't what to talk about." Willie said.

Right then and there I fell into silence.

SAN JUAN HILL

Every so often Sleepy Willie likes to talk about his old San Juan Hill neighborhood in midtown Manhattan. It's the first place he lived when he came to New York City, from Beaufort, South Carolina. Or, as Willie likes to put it, when he fled the brutal South for the mean streets of New York City. Last weekend, Willie attended his neighborhood's three-day reunion. His periodic melancholy for his old stomping grounds was evident in everything he said this evening.

"Half of the old-timers from the old neighborhood showed up," Willie said about the reunion.

"What happened to the other half," I asked.

"Death." Willie said. "Let me put it another way. Half of the people from the neighborhood who are alive were there. There are some people I didn't see there over the weekend, who I know are still alive and living here in the city. But it was still the best three days I've had in a long time. Ecaroh, let me tell you, we rehashed some great memories. You would have to know what kind of community San Juan Hill was back in the forties, fifties, and early sixties to appreciate the whole experience."

"Well I certainly feel like I know some of those folks, as much as you talk about them. San Juan Hill is where the Amsterdam Housing Projects are. Thelonious Monk lived there and. . . ."

"Monk didn't live in the projects," Willie protested.

"I didn't mean he lived in the projects."

"Monk lived on Sixty-third Street. A street that is now named Thelonious Sphere Monk Circle," Willie said.

"I've been down there with you on more than one occasion. Lincoln Center was built right across from the projects on Amsterdam Avenue. I still remember some of your funny stories about the Bar you called Gun Smoke Café."

"Well I'm not going retell any of those stories tonight. A hand full of guys my age and a few old ladies were there. But there were maybe a hundred and fifty of the younger people. Black, Puerto Ricans, and a few whites."

"I'm not surprised that the reunion was mixed, but it knocks me out that there were that many guys your age still around," I said.

"Funny. We are a community of close knit people with a good survival rate. We didn't have the kind of friction in our neighborhood that kills people before their time. I have to say that there were crazy times. Some of the guys had us all cracking up about a headline that was in *The Daily News* back in the mid-fifties. Some young boys from the projects went row boating in Central Park. On the lake they came upon a group of well-to-do boys, also row boating. There was a little altercation between the two groups of boys and the boys from our neighborhood left the lake with some belongings of the boys they came upon. This happened on a Friday, somebody remembered. The headline in *The Daily News* that Saturday read *Piracy on the High Sea*. It was probably a slow news day. But I remember the whole community got quite a kick out of it. Those boys got in some trouble with the law. But they were treated like celebrities in the neighborhood because they brought some notoriety to our community. We all had a good laugh about that incident."

"Then this really wasn't what you would call the ideal community. Not with that kind of notoriety."

"Oh, we had all the kinds of problems other poor working class black neighborhoods in the city had. We had youth gangs, drugs, crime and all that stuff. There was a boy in the neighbor called Polly Wolly; he was what is called a ghetto star today. He was a charismatic bad boy with charm and heart, and the other youths look up to him. When he was in the Youthhouse one of his many times, the thugs there commissioned him to organize the Sportsman street gang in our neighborhood. Shortly after that period marijuana and heroin use became more visible in our community. His boys had names like Wine, Superman, Dittybop, Stonewall Jackson, Graveyard, Hip, and that kind of thing. But this all was in the background. We were a community that remained hopeful. And at that time, before the world became so cynical, I think location had something to do with the success of our community. We were in a part of the city where we could see how other people lived. From Sixty-second Street we could see the possibilities. From midtown, the youth of our community could envision one day getting out of town. We were in walking distance to the Museum of Natural History and the Planetarium. We had Central Park for our front yard and Riverside Park for our back yard. We were exposed to all the activities of the 59ᵗʰ street Coliseum and the old Madison Square Garden. Our youth could see that there was hope. The vision wasn't so close and clear from other parts of the city. The children from that period of San Juan Hill became writers, artists, actors, politicians, lawyers, priest, you name it."

"So what happened to kill the spirit of San Juan Hill, and make it what it is today Willie?"

"They called it the Amsterdam/Lincoln Square Community these days."

"You're not telling me that the community took a downturn because the name changed?"

"I don't know."

"Oh, come on Willie."

"No. There's more to it than that. It could be that as the successful young people found their niche and moved away, they took all the hope with them. All they left behind was the hopeless. You know there are still some people living there now who lived there fifty years ago. There is a guy who's been hanging out in the playground on Sixty-fourth Street since it was built in the late forties. I mean how hip is it to be hanging in a playground for over fifty years? A couple of generations have grown up there, spent a few years in the playground and moved on. Even I have moved from that playground in mid-Manhattan to this bar in The Bronx."

"I thought you were talking about making moves that are improvements," I said.

"I am." Willie said. "Plenty things have happened to me between the playground and Two Cousins Bar, things good and bad. And forty years of experience."

"Well Willie, I'm extremely happy about all of your many experiences and that you come from a neighborhood like no other in all the earth, but I've got to make it home now."

"Don't be like that," Willie said, "the night is young and I'm enjoying our talk. Let me buy you a beer?"

"No man, as hard an offer as this is to refuse, coming from you on this rare occasion, I think I've had enough tonight. Enough beer and enough San Juan Hill."

"San Juan Hill wasn't the greatest neighborhood in the world, I don't think, not even the greatest in America, or in New York City. It just happens to have been a damn good place to live back in those old days. That's all I'm saying. I was there and I wanted you to know about it."

STICK-UP MEN

"Can't stay long tonight," Sleepy Willie said, just as I sat down.

"Why? You don't have a date," I said starting off tonight's talk on a playful note. Then I ordered two beers. My way of saying to Willie that I didn't believe him about not staying long. He would be there until we had talked ourselves out and was out of beer money.

"I wish having a date was the reason," Willie said, a downcast in his voice. "Last Friday-night I stayed a while after you left—guess I got home around twelve, twelve-thirty. Whatever time it was, it was the wrong time. I got mugged in my own hallway."

"What! I don't believe you didn't call me. Man I just. . . ."

"Call you for what. There was nothing you could do. I did make out a police report although I know that there ain't nothing they can do."

"Man, I'm glad they didn't hurt you," I said. "These young hoodlums today get off hurting people."

"No, they didn't harm me, not physically anyway. But my feeling and my pride as a man who can take care of himself took a real beating. I'm hurt that these bums are forcing me to restrict my movements and my behavior."

"How did it happen? Do you feel up to talking about it?"

"Getting home safe at night is serious business in the ghetto.

I'm usually careful and alert. I look for the slightest thing that doesn't seem right. I can't say where my mind was this night. It might have been that I was too tired and sleepy."

"I know what you are saying," I said.

"Anyway," Willie continued, "I got to my block alright. I wasn't thinking trouble. God knows anything can happen at any time in these mean streets of the South Bronx. These young hoodlums are mighty vicious. Some of them would steal from their own mamas and I know it. This night my urban survival instincts flew out the window. When I reached my building I took my keys out and unlocked the vestibule door. I opened the door and notice that the hall light was out. It was then that the light in my head came on. Something is up, but it was too late. Soon as I opened the door two hoods inside the darkened vestibule snatched the door wide open and pulled me inside. At the same time another one, who must have hidden outside, grabbed me from behind. The two in front held knives, one in my face, the other in my belly. The hood behind me pushed something in my back that could have been a gun. It felt like a gun. 'Don't be no hero,' the hood behind me said."

"Sounds like these cats were serious," I said

"Then he called me an old fool which made me mad. I could tell that I was smarter then the three of them. After all, they were the ones dumb enough to have to stick-up an old man smart enough to have eight dollars and thirty cents of his own money in his pocket. I asked them what they wanted. The boy behind me, who I figured to be the leader because he was smart enough to stay out of sight said, my wallet would do."

"So you got looks at two of them."

"I took good looks at the two in front of me with knives. They were between fifteen and nineteen years old with bright innocent eyes and clean faces. I gave up my wallet with the eight dollars in it. I felt a great sense of despair for them. Really, I did, even as they robbed me. These are young boys who would pass through life without ever having a chance at living. Society and their parents have dealt them such a dirty hand. These are kids who under better conditions could make something of themselves. That's why I felt sorry for them."

"Well that's mighty big of you," I said, "but I can't see sympathy for stick-up men or boys."

"What you got to say, the guy behind asked. Well you know that is when he made his big mistake—asking me to talk. I didn't talk to answer him; I talked to educate him. I told them about the eight dollars in my wallet and why I was its rightful owner. I told them that they were stealing less from me than had been stolen from them. Yeah, I did. I told them about how their parents robbed them of a basic sense of decency and the self-esteem that would have given them the ability to succeed in life. I told them about the educational system that robbed them of the knowledge to gain a repectable place in society. I'm losing eight dollars tonight, for me that is a small lost, compared to what's been stolen from you three."

"You said all that with what could have been a gun in your back?"

"But that's not all I told them. I talked about politicians who stick them up by short changing their community and make laws favoring the rich and powerful. I told them about state governors who stick them up by using the tax money of hard working common people to build bigger and better jails; jails that they would some day experience. Then I told them about educated stick-up men; stock speculators and the Wall Street muggers who manipulate the economy and steal millions of dollars everyday. The health industry is a stick-up game, lawyer's stick-up people all the time. There is lots of stealing going on. Some stick-up men steal eight dollars others steal eight million. The deal is this: you need an education to do any big-time stick-ups. Look at the bankers that stuck-up the United States taxpayers for four hundred billion dollars in the saving and loan scandals back in the Reagan era. Okay, so they got help from the Whitehouse and the Congress, but they still had to be educated people to pull this stick-up off. These bankers didn't start their stick-up careers in darken hallways, they got their start in brightly lit school classrooms. This hallway thing is for losers who end up in the big prisons that stealing politicians build."

"Man, you're lucky to make it out of the hallway alive talking like that to hoodlum."

"The fact that they listened to all of this made me think that I had impressed them. I could almost hear their minds grinding over what I had said to them. The thing that felt like a gun was no longer pressed against my back. Then I said, kind of sympathetically, while you are stealing eight dollars from me, your future is being stolen from you. All I'm trying to do is pull your coat to the truth."

"Well what happened?" I asked.

Sleepy Willie took his wallet out. He took a five and three ones from it. "Two more beers," Willie shouted to the barmaid, "I've got eight dollars to spend."

4496-MUNG

WILLIE SINGS THE BLUES

The owners of the Two Cousins Bar run a successful enterprise. A small part of that success is the music on their jukebox. They keep a good selection of classic mainstream jazz, lots of blues, and some contemporary hits in their jukebox. It's the music to set the right ambience for the mature crowd that patronizes the bar. Here·is what was playing last week when I sat down to talk with Sleepy Willie:

I ain't good looking and my hair ain't curl/ain't good looking and my hair ain't curl/but my mother she gave me something it's gonna carry me through this world/some men like me 'cause I'm happy/some 'cause I'm snappy/some call me honey/others think I've got money/some tell me Billie, baby you built for speed/now when you put that all together makes me everything a good man needs.

When the Billie Holiday record ended a hip-hop record began to play.

"When is the last time you heard a new and exciting blues tune from someone who can make you feel the words?" Sleepy Willie asked.

"I can't remember," I said. "Blues as an art form is lost. I mean traditional blues. You can hear some of the words and sentiments in some of the music these kids are making today, but traditional blues, that old get it out of your system, tell it all, go to church blues is dead."

"The blues ain't dead," Willie said, " can't be."

"I don't know Willie, my guess is that there just isn't an audience for that kind of music any more. Young people today listen to what you hear on the box now. Listen at it."

"The blues may have fallen back," Willie said, "but it ain't dead. People study the blues as an art form. The blues is taught in colleges as a part of American music history. The blues is too important a part of the musical tradition of black America to die completely. Blues ain't just a musical art form; it's a link in the living history of American black folks. Do you know that the first Africans on the slave's ships to the Americas sent up a wail-beseeching god for something that would fortify them and give them perseverance to withstand the coming years of bondage and hardships. God heard them, but they had nothing, they were naked and in chains, so God took the only thing they had, the very sound of their wail, and fashioned it into their sword and their shield. Today we call that sound music. And it is that wail, in its ever-developing forms that have nurtured us through three centuries of hell on earth. The blues is a middle link in our musical development. I like to think that that first wail was the first note of the blues."

"Willie, there are times when you just blow my mind. That's a beautiful concept, if there were more people who felt this deeply about the blues there wouldn't be any danger of losing the music."

"This young generation may not be up on the blues, but it's still played on the radio. You just have to search for it. Plus there are some sections of the country where the blues is still strong."

"I don't know how you would know what music is popular outside of New York City, you haven't left the city since you arrived and that was before the last big war. Fact is, its become impossible to get you out of the South Bronx."

"What you talking about man," Willie said, "I read Down Beat and Blues Magazines, and I listen to Ruth Brown's radio program on WBGO to keep up with what's happening. Let me tell you, Chicago puts New York to shame when it comes to keeping the blues alive. In Chicago there are many blues clubs in the nightlife section of town and a few of the real deal on the Southside of Chicago. The blues is doing well down in the South. Many Southern cities hold weeklong blues festivals with live appearances by current blues stars. Why, even white boys sing the blues these days. I never told you this, but I have written a blues song or two myself."

"You have," I said somewhat astonished, "Willie, you've been holding out on me."

"You don't have to know everything about me, nobody does."

"Well, one thing for sure," I said, "You've lived the kind of life that should have generated a lot of material for your blues songs."

"There is probably one good blues song in every life," Willie said, "I've got a whole show-book out of mine."

"Have you sent any of your blues songs to record companies or blues artists?"

"No."

"Why not man? Are you just writing for yourself?"

"There are very few cats out there today that could do justice to my songs. There ain't many people who would appreciate them for what they are. Why people today don't even appreciate the great classic blues lines."

"Run one by me," I said.

Willie thought for a moment then he offered:

You told me when we first met/that your life was awful tame/ then I took you to a nightclub/and the whole band knew your name.

"I like that," I said. "Few words that speak volumes about betrayal and the loose life. Who wouldn't appreciate the irony in that metaphor?"

Right then a contemporary rap-tune entered our consciousness with:

You lick me and I'll lick you/'cause we're kicking it/with licking it.

"You don't want to listen to that kind of stuff all your life," Willie said. "Try this on for size:

*I'm gonna move baby way on the outta skirts of town/you see
I don't need nobody always hanging 'round/let me tell you honey
we gone move away from here/I don't need no iceman gonna get
you a frigidaire/when we move on the out skirts of town/we don't
need nobody always hanging 'round.*

"I've heard that one. I know it's an old standard, but I think
I heard it sung by Ray Charles."

"Yeah, you've heard it by Brother Ray and he sings it well,
but when I think about that song I hear the Jimmy Rushing,
Count Basie version. I can see big Jimmy Rushing bellowing out:

*Now it may sound funny honey/funny as can be/if we have a
dozen children/you know they all gone look like me/when we move
way back of town/we don't need nobody always hanging 'round.*

"The blues is poetry in style and content," Willie said. "The
blues talked about love and love lost. The blues talked about
oppression, concession, recession, and suppression. The blues
talked about Jim Crow and high times. The blues talked about
having a full belly and hard times. The blues is history; the history of African descendants in these United States. The blues is
that version of American history that ain't taught in schools. God
turned the first wail of the first slaves into their sword and shield,
and we turned the blues into our history book."

Willie was absolutely aglow. He was talking about something
he loved and knew well. I had him in my hands as far as this
subject was concerned; I could make him sing like a bird. "Let's
hear another verse of something?" I asked.

Listen to this:

*Hey everybody lets have some fun/you only live but once/and
when you dead you done/so let the good times roll/I say let the
good times roll/I don't care if you're young or old/I say let the
good times roll/everybody Sleepy Willie's in town/got a dollar and
a quarter and I'm rearing to clown/but don't let no female play me
cheap/I got fifty cent more then I'm gonna keep/so let the good
times roll.*

"You see," Willie continued, "the blue could be jolly fun or deadly serious. Have you ever heard Louis Armstrong sing 'What Did I Do To Be So Black and Blue?'"

"No, but I've read Ralph Ellison's book Invisible Man. In the book there is this long passage where the protagonist smoked a joint that he thought was a regular cigarette and played that Armstrong record and had a surreal experience that took him back throughout the time of slavery."

"Deadly serious," Willie said. Talking about deadly serious—have you ever heard Billy Holiday sing 'Strange Fruit?'"

"No, I've got that by Nina Simone. It's a song about a deadly serious time in our history. My turn—do you remember Ruth Brown's 'Mamma He Treats Your Daughter Mean?'"

"1952," Willie said. "Ruth Brown made it big at the end of the Louie Jordan era. Louie Jordan dominated the charts from after the war until the early fifties. Ruth was big, but it was a cat name Charles Brown who knocked Louie Jordan off the top ten charts. Do you know who Charles Brown is?"

"Charles Brown—I don't think so. What are we doing Willie, playing blues trivia."

"Every Christmas for the last forty some odd years, radio stations across the country play a Charles Brown Christmas song that is as widely known in our communities as Bing Crosby's 'White Christmas' is around the world."

"You don't mean 'Merry Christmas Baby?'"

Willie sang:

Santa came down the chimney half past three/bought all these presents for my baby and for me/ Merry Christmas baby/you sho' did treat me right.

"Oh! That's Charles Brown. I never knew who sung that song, but I've heard it every Christmas since I can remember."

"As long as there is Christmas," Willie said, " 'Merry Christmas Baby' will be on the air."

"You know Willie, hearing all those fine blues lyrics you recited here tonight has heightened my interest in hearing some of your original blues tunes. I want to hear William Walker sing the blues."

"The closest you'll come to that is hearing the lyrics of a song that could have been written for me. This is a song about the survival of some young Southern girls who came North."

"Willie, you're Southern and when you came North you were young, but you were not female. So how is a song written for you?"

"Picture Big Mabel on the stage at the Apollo Theater and listen to these words she's singing:

My ice man is a nice man/just as nice as he can be/'cause he goes collects his money/and he bring it all to me/and my wood man is a good man 'cause he likes to keep me warm/when his wood don't burn to suit me/then he takes me in his arms/and my meat man is a sweet man/brings me chicken everyday/then he tells me pretty baby you don't never have to pay/and my landlord he done told me not to worry 'bout the rent/all he wants to do is hold me/and my rent won't cost a cent/now my coal man is an old man/ almost eighty-two/but believe me when I tell you/he sho' know what to do.

"I've been the ice man, the wood man, the coal man and the old man to many a young thing in my days," Willie said. "Yeah there are lyrics of the blues that capture the life of William Walker."

"Willie I have to leave in a few, before I go how about a cold one on me?"

"That would be nice," Willie said.

"First let me hear some of your own lyrics," I demand.

"Who do you think I am?" Sleepy Willie snarled. "I don't sing the blues for a pig's foot nor a bottle of beer."

THE REUNION

I rushed over to Sleepy Willie's apartment as soon as I heard the word. Willie let me in and walked back to the kitchen table where he had been sipping coffee and listening to Mahalia Jackson's recording of "In the Upper Room."

"You heard man," I said rather emotionally, as I sat down. "Dr. Betty Shabazz is gone."

"Yeah, I heard," Willie said, "just like I dreamt last night. But you can leave me to my joy, if you can't get those tears out of your eyes."

"Who's playing that sad sounding Mahalia Jackson song?"

"Interpretation and perception is everything. That's not a sad song. That's a song about the final victory. You know, I'm worried that some people will misinterpret Sister Betty's passing and miss the victory of her life and death."

"How's that? Willie how should we view the death of Dr. Shabazz?"

"Like it was in my dream."

"And how was that?"

"In my dream, *Sister Betty ascends to a cloud filled spot in the unknown and is met by Brother Malcolm. Their eyes merged and they remained speechless as both kneeled toward the east in prayer. Brother Malcolm was tall and rested. Sister Betty was even more radiant then she was in life. Then, for the first time in more than thirty years, they embraced. There were still no words, as they held each other. Words were not necessary in this moment; in this paradise.*

"Then Malcolm led Betty to a consecrated spot where they sat under a shining gazebo in a blissful gaze. Lions romped in the distance among the lambs. Brother Malcolm spoke the first words.'My dear beloved, my dearest Betty, at long last we are re-united in this everlasting rapture. I eagerly waited your arrival knowing that the day would come when your earthly mission would be completed. My beloved, it is good to see you. I craved the very essence of you.' Then Malcolm smiled and the birds chirped and the air was sanctified.

"They sat in that exalted timelessness holding hands as Malcolm explained the welcoming banquet to come. The Heav-enly Host would be seated at the head of the table. In seats of honor to the right and left, would be Martin Luther King Jr. and Megar Evers. There would be an opening selection by Ella Fitzgerald, followed by opening remarks from Thurgood Marshall. Zora Neale Hurston would make the main address. Then there will be a grand presentation from The Almighty. Adam Clayton Powell Jr. would give the benediction. Sara Vaughn would make the closing selection.

"Sister Betty seemed pleased with the banquet plans, but Malcolm sensed that her mind had gone on to earthly matters. She still held concerns for those left behind. And he said, 'None of that can distress you now my dearest. Our dear daughters, our family, and our friends will grieve for a while, but the time will come when they will reach an understanding acceptance My dear Betty, even our detractors will honor your ascension. I know that your greatest concern is for young Malcolm. Martin Luther King Jr. has become young Malcolm's guardian angel. Martin will guide Malcolm to peace, redemption, and a productive life of service. Everything will work out, my beloved.' Malcolm smiled a radiant smile and Sister Betty smiled back knowingly. The birds and the lions and the lambs romped in benevolence.

"And I woke up this morning knowing that an important leader is gone. But I also know that she is with Malcolm, and that makes me feel good. I can glorify the many blessings she has given to so many people. Her life was a life well spent," Sleepy Willie said as he poured me a cup of coffee. Then he walked over to the record player and put the Mahalia Jackson record on continuous play.

PEOPLE WILLIE LOVES TO HATE

"Lots of the joy goes out of life when people I love to hate leave the public arena," Sleepy Willie said.

"I left my safety helmet home," I answered, "but hit me with it any how."

"Well maybe hate is too strong a word," Willie said. "Maybe I should say people I love to criticize. Lots of my favorite characters have vanished from the public arena and I miss them sorely. You know the kind of people I mean, people who make life miserable for black folks, but in doing so make it easier for some of us to focus on where the race question is going."

"Willie, I've known you for years and I know that you're capable of almost any emotion, but missing people who dispensed misery—come on."

"I've been around for a long time," Willie said. "I've seen just about everything you can imagine on the question of race. This country has produced some pretty good people who wanted to do the right thing about racial equality and I've admired them. This country has also produced some racial antagonists. Tonight I want to remember the bad folks—the one who kept me focused on the prize. I'd really like to know what happened to them all. How life is going with them these days."

"What you really want to know," I said, "is if what goes around comes around."

"That's right,' Willie said. "I want to know if some of the misery they dished out ever caught up to them."

"Willie do you feel comfortable with these kinds of vindictive feelings?"

"I know the fate of some of them," Willie said, brushing my question aside. "You take a guy like Clarence Pendelton—remember him?"

"No, I can't say that I do. Who is he and why do you hate him?"

"Clarence is dead now. May God bless his soul. He was a small Negro, who was appointed Chairman of the Civil Rights Commission by Ronald Reagan. Where they find these Negroes I'll never know. When there is dirty work to be done to black Americans, they can always find an employable Negro. Anyway, Reagan gave Pendelton the Civil Rights Commission job and the assignment to convince the Congress and the American people that there was no longer a need for a Civil Rights Commission. I know it's funny, but don't laugh. Reagan gave this Negro a job, then gave him the mission of abolishing his own job."

"He must not have been very effective," I said, "the Civil Rights Commission still exist."

"Still exist," Willie laughed, "and out of danger. But I've got to be fair to Clarence, because it wasn't like he didn't give it his best shot. He made some headlines—brought some attention to the issue. It was Clarence Pendelton who first told America the lie that the white male population is the most discriminated against group in America. You might say that it was old Clarence, a brown skin Negro, who fathered the angry white male movement of the early nineties. Well, you know, old Clarence was married to a white gal, so maybe he was more familiar with the white man's burden than I knew."

"Boy are you tough on that dead man," I said.

"There is another dead man on my list. A man who was so powerful, he was feared by crime kings, subversives, murders, bank robbers, and presidents."

"Presidents? Willie, who could make an American president, fear him. You must mean presidents of Caribbean Island countries?"

"Them too, but I'm talking about American presidents. And the person is none other than J. Edgar Hoover, the head of the Federal Bureau of Investigation—the FBI."

"Why did you hate . . . oops, why is Hoover on your list?"

"For the way he treated African Americans—our leaders and organizations. Hoover used to say that our quest for equality was communist inspired. I found that highly insulting. He could find a communist on the moon, but he couldn't find all the terrorist who bombed that church and killed those little girls in Alabama. Why that sucker had the audacity to try to get Martin Luther King to commit suicide. Hoover had the dope on everybody and he would use it too. Now we find out that Hoover was a faggot. Man when I first heard that I laughed so hard I cried."

"Why," I asked, "because he was gay? Willie, it's not hip any more, to make fun of gay people. It's not politically correct."

"Politically correct," Willie began to laugh, "no, no, that's not why I laughed. Tha, tha, that's not why I'm laughing now."

Sleepy Willie was now laughing uncontrollably. I watched and waited for him to calm down.

"It's the irony," Willie laughed. America's toughest G-man, a man feared by presidents because of the sexual dirt he had on them, had a bedroom filled with his own dirt—taboo dirt at that. Man that's ironic and funny as hell."

"Next," I said.

"What about old George?"

"George who?"

"George 'ain't a dimes worth of difference between 'um' Wallace."

"Who?"

"George Wallace, who use to be governor of Alabama during the movement time. First he used racism to build a political career in Alabama, and then George built two national presidential campaigns on racism before a young white boy shot him up. I tell you, Don King was the best at using racism to promote boxing matches. George Wallace was king at using racism in politics.

Nixon and Reagan learned a thing or two from the Wallace campaigns. Wallace was a media racist. He manipulated the Justice Department into nationalizing the Alabama National Guard, while he stood in the doorway of the University of Alabama. The world's news cameras captured a lone George Wallace defending the institutions of whiteness from the invasion of blackness. Bigots all over America got that message. If it wasn't for the bullets of a would be assassin, in sixty-eight, Nixon would not have been the one."

"Do you really think that Wallace could have been elected," I asked.

"Wallace's campaign slogan was 'SENT THEM A MESSAGE'. He was hoping that enough white voters would vote the message of white backlash for him to win the Democratic nomination. George was pulling large crowds at his political rallies—even in the North, then one of five bullets paralyzed old George from the waist down. It was all over—life ain't ever been the same for George Wallace. Over time, George, like the Grinch who stole Christmas, found out that his heart was two sizes too small. He stood in the doorway of history and the civil rights movement rolled him over."

"Didn't he go to Martin Luther King's church and apologized for all the trouble he caused black people and the nation? He became a completely repentant man and in his final years in power in Alabama, he put blacks in his government, as well as, awarded black owned companies state contracts."

"Oh yes," Sleepy Willie answered, "he did all of that—fact is—he even won an election with a majority of the black vote. We are a forgiving people. We think it is the highest christian gift to be able to forgive. But, you know, between the old George and the new George, there wasn't a dimes worth of difference. And he died that way."

I looked at my watch. It was getting late, but Willie was having too much fun for me to leave him just yet.

"You got a date somewhere?" Willie asked

"No, man. I just don't want to let the time get away from me. Now tell me, who is next on your miss list?"

"Ronald Reagan. I miss him, but I'm glad he's gone. The whole country ought to be glad that that cat is gone. Ronald Reagan gave the country to rich white men while poor to average white folks applauded. Some white folks are strange. Rush Limbaugh eats a banquet and they're full, Limbaugh accumulates a fortune and they feel rich. Ronald Reagan empowered the powerful and the poor working stiff felt powerful."

"Ronald Reagan was an extremely popular president," I said. "He had the full confidence of white America. He made them feel good and he was doing what they wanted done—and that was to move the country away from the social spending of the past. He was the icon for the conservative mood in the country."

"Ronald Reagan was a sophisticated George Wallace when it came to the question of race. He subtlety signaled those same sentiments that Wallace growled. The message whites got from Reagan was 'I'm going to stick it to them and look out for us.' The joke is that he stuck it to average white folk too. They are so happy when we get stepped on that they are blind to what happens to them. Conservative politicians know this fact well, they are polish slick when it comes to manipulating race. Ronald Reagan was a rich white man's dream and a poor man's nightmare. Man I miss Reagan. I'm glad to miss him."

"Willie it's getting late."

"Order a couple, while I wrap this up."

"I think it's your turn, my man."

"I also miss those days when you didn't pay attention to who bought the last round of beers. That was before Reagan created the four trillion-dollar national debt."

There was a moment of silence. Then:

"Rose, bring one cold one to this table," Willie called out.

"Oh, I see," I said, "you're going to buy a beer for yourself huh?"

"That one's for you. Now let me tell you who I miss most."

"Rose," I hollered out, "bring two beers—my tab. Who Willie?"

"Edward I. Koch."

"Miss Koch—why?"

"Miss Koch," Willie laughed, "are you trying to say something?"

"Willie, I know what you're alluding too. Don't put that on me because I don't know a thing about Koch beyond his years as mayor of New York City."

"Well I'm sure you remember the mayoralty race between Mario Cuomo and Koch."

"Yeah. I voted for Cuomo—Koch won."

"It was a close race down to the final days. Some of Cuomo's people drove through some neighborhoods with their bullhorns telling people to 'VOTE FOR CUOMO NOT THE HOMO' they knew something about Koch the public didn't."

"Koch still won," I said.

"And he won two other times," Willie answered. "This is New York City."

Rose brought the beers. Willie handed her two empty bottles. He poured his glass full from the new bottle and took a sip.

"Two things Willie, first you don't like Koch because you think he's gay. Second, if you're a Koch watcher you couldn't be missing him. He's been all over the place since his days at City Hall. Koch has been a commentator on television, a newspaper columnist and he's been a judge on The People's Court."

"I don't have anything against being a Homo. It was his side-ways racism that got to me, not his sexual preference. Koch set a racial atmosphere that took the city down an ugly path. He wasn't the mayor of all the people; he was guarding the gate for some of the people. Yeah, you're right, Koch didn't go away quietly into the night. But the difference is his powerlessness. And that's what I'm celebrating tonight, the powerlessness of the people I love to hate."

"Well if that's the end of your list I'm gonna leave now."

"I did want to mention the new crop coming up. That's the one thing I can always depend on . . . there is always another crop moving onto the stage."

BREAST FED PRESIDENTS

"Interesting, very interesting," Sleepy Willie said as he placed the Health section of *The New York Times,* he had been reading down on our table at the Two Cousins Bar. He took a sip from his beer and looked out of the window deep in thought.

"What's interesting, very interesting?" I asked.

"This article in the papers," Willie said. "It's about a study published in the *New England Journal of Medicine.* The study found that people who were breast-fed turn out to be better-adjusted adults than people who were not. According to this study, the bonding that takes place during the first months of life improves positive personality development. The quality of early bonding determines future adult evolution. The study says that people who were breast-fed are more self assured, less aggressive, less hostile, more compassionate, and generally more congruous than people who were not breast-fed. The study looked at the lives of hundreds of people from all walks of life. The people who conducted the study over twenty years, interviewed people in government, business, education, entertainment, sports, blue collar worker, and even jail inmates. There were whites, Hispanics, Asian, and us."

"Willie, you might find this interesting," I said, "but surely not important. I mean what does one do with such information?"

"Change the world, that's all," Willie said excitedly. "If all it takes to create well adjusted compassionate, amicable people is a few months of breast suckling, in a generation we can change the world."

"Willie, people have breast-fed from the beginning of time and what has that brought us?"

"It's the non-breast feeders among us that turn out to be societies maulers. In the last sixty years or so, the non-breast feeders have grown to out number the breast feeders. This is the source of our present debacle. But all that can change with something as simple as increased breast bonding. Oh yes, women's breast shall change the world," Sleepy Willie sang.

"Man, you sound like you're willing to bet the farm on this study. What proof do you have that any of the studies claims are true?"

"You are looking at living proof."

"Oh, you were breast fed?"

"Can't you tell," Willie said. "You have never met a more well adjusted, self-assured, and sociable human in all the South Bronx. I come from a time when breast-feeding was natural and common . . . and necessary. But more than that, I come from a place where breast-feeding was sometimes communal."

"Communal breast-feeding, come on Willie, sometimes I think that you think that you can shoot any line to me and I'll suck it all in."

"Shortly after my birth," Willie said, "my mother went back to work at the cigar factory in Beaufort, so we could only breast bond in the early mornings and late evenings. My mother had a first cousin that had a baby a few weeks younger than I was. During the day, my grandmother would take me to my mother's cousin's house who breast-fed me and her own child—often at the same time. To this day me and my cousin whose mama breast-fed us together are as close as twins and he's got his things as together as I have mine. He too, is a well adjusted adult."

"Yeah," I said, "and right now he's sitting in some bar in South Carolina talking about his well-adjusted cousin in the South Bronx."

"Wherever he is, he's okay, I'm sure. But my point is that this was a common thing back in those days among the Coastal Island people of North and South Carolina, and the coastal sections of Georgia. I believe that this is a tradition that somehow these people retained from our African past. Communal breast feeding is one of the traditions that could come from the saying 'It takes a village to raise a child.' "

"Willie, you and I have been having these conversations for many years now. Twice a week I expose myself to your views no matter how outrageous. But this thing about breast-feeding is got to top them all. I mean. . . ."

"Just think how different things could have been," Willie interrupted, " why the history of the modern world could have been altered if some of the world's tyrants had been breast-fed. Imagine how different things could be right here in the South Bronx, if more of our neighborhood head-knockers had been breast-fed. I'd be able to walk the streets safely at night. I say breast-feeding should be more than encouraged—there ought to be a law. But this thing goes farther than that. What are the qualifications to be president of the United States?"

"As far as I know, the constitution only requires that the person be thirty-five years old and be a natural born citizen," I answered.

"That's the two written qualifications," Willie said, "but there are two unwritten qualifications."

"Oh," I said, "what are they?"

"That the president be white and that he be male."

"That's the way it's been to this point, but that will change," I said.

"I would like to add another requirement, but I don't want it to be an unwritten requirement like the white/male thing. I want it to be a written constitutional requirement that no one shall become president of the United States, who is not thirty-five years of age, a natural born citizen, and breast-fed."

"Breast-fed?"

"Yes, breast-fed. Look—if breast-fed people are more compassionate, more spiritually harmonious, even smarter than people who are not breast-fed, why shouldn't we require that anyone wanting to be president be breast-fed? We should take it all the way by requiring that anyone seeking any position of responsibility, from president on down, produce a breast-fed certificate."

"Willie, this all makes sense in a kind of crazy way, but then, what else should I expect from you. Let me play with this idea for a minute. How do you know that none of our past presidents had been breast-fed?"

"Oh I'm sure that some of the early presidents from common households, like Lincoln, were probably breast-fed. But of the recent presidents the only ones I'd bet were breast-fed are Jimmy Carter, Truman, and maybe, just maybe, Bill Clinton."

"Oh, I'm sure Clinton was breast-fed," I joked, "if not in infancy, at some later date."

"I know that none of the presidents who came from rich families were breast-fed. All those cats had nannies and probably had to make appointments to see their mamas. I don't believe you can get a compassionate, caring person out of such a situation, much less a caring compassionate president."

"Richard Nixon didn't come from a rich family. Do you think he was breast-fed?"

"No," Willie said, "Richard Nixon ain't never displayed any traits that would suggest that he even knew what a breast is."

"That's cold," I said.

"I tell you," Willie continued, "Women's breast will save the world as soon as every mother, everywhere, turn to breast-feeding. It's a time that is sure to come."

"You really think so?"

"Yeah. It's just a shame that nothing can be done for all the millions of grown people who were not breast-fed. It's just too bad that the benefits of breast-feeding can't be had retroactively."

"And it's a good thing too," I said, "because I'm sure you would come up with a program to get grown men breast-fed."

"I would do what I could to bring peace to the world and to the South Bronx," Sleepy Willie said, then went back to reading the newspaper.

WHITES ONLY

Last week my cousin Allison and his wife were in town from South Carolina, to spend a week with my wife and me. All during the week we took them over much of the city. We went a top the World Trade Center. We spent a day at the Metropolitan Museum of Art. We dined at Silvia's in Harlem and visited the Shomburg library. We saw a show at the Apollo Theater and drove out to City Island for seafood. We took the subway to shop at Macy's and Bloomindales. We did all of this and more, but the visit Allison anticipated more than any other was the Friday evening stop at Two Cousins Bar in the South Bronx, to drink and talk with Sleepy Willie. I talked Willie up so much, that I may have muted Allison's appreciation of the events of the early week.

Friday evening Allison and I arrived at the bar in good spirits. I flung the door open and with my cousin in tow, walked a prideful strive to the table where Sleepy Willie sat sipping an imported one. Willie rose as he noticed us approaching. Willie and I embraced and I introduced him to Allison, whom, Willie also hugged. We all sat down. Rosa, the barmaid came over to say hello. "So you're Ecaroh's cousin from South Carolina. I've heard so much about you," Rosa lied. "What can I bring you?"

"Bring us a round of beers," Willie said. "That's alright with you," he asked Allison, who nodded in agreement. In less time than I ever experience, Rosa was back with three imported

beers. She was on her best behavior—I hoped Willie would
be too.

" Have you and your wife been treated to a good time in the
city?" Willie asked.

"Man they took us every place," Allison said. "We been
downtown, uptown and all around. New York City is a big
place with lots of excitement. Man I just don't know how you
folks don't burst from all the things to do—and I mean all the
time."

"We manage," said Willie, a man who rarely leaves the South
Bronx. "When are you going back?"

"Sunday morning," Allison answered.

"If you weren't going back so soon, I'd take you around to
see my New York," Willie said.

"Your New York," I said, "we're in half of your New York
right now. The other half of your New York is your apartment on
Sherman Avenue."

"I have a New York that's unique to me," Willie said." A
more then fifty year perspective on places, events and people."

"I hear that you're from down home," Allison asked Willie,
slicing through the playful tension between Willie and myself.

"Something I ain't particular proud of," Willie said, creating
a real tension at our table.

"I'm been trying to convince Willie that South Carolina has
come a long way in race relations," I said, "things aren't like
they were when he lived there."

"That's right," Allison said. "The most controversial race
problem in South Carolina is probably that they still fly the
Confederate flag on the state grounds after taking it down from
the Statehouse. There are other problems concerning race, but
this flag thing is the one that really pushed everybody's hot button,
especially white people's."

"That's because that flag is their last bastion of symbolic white
onlyism," Willie said.

"Huh." Allison said.

"Now you'll see what I've been telling you about this man," I said to Allison.

"White folks in South Carolina are losing a feel of who they use to be," Willie said. "They're in transition from one social understanding to another. They feel the need to cling to the familiar. When they had slavery they knew who they were. Then segregation gave them a sense of loftiness. Jim Crow laws and whites only water fountains helped them to feel good about themselves right up into the late sixties. Now all that is gone, so they hold on to the only thing left that gives them a sense of group identity and somebodyness. A somebodyness separate and above the black population."

"Willie, are you saying that flying the Confederate flag nourish some kind of mass psychological deficiency in white South Carolinians?" I asked.

" It comforts them," Willie said, "it's the only link left."

"Link to what?" I asked.

"Their heritage," Willie said. Those folks in South Carolina who still need to fly the Confederate flag are folks who still need something to replace the whites only water fountains—something that in their minds—unites and elevates them above the other people in the state."

"Well they do say it's heritage and not hate on their bumper stickers," Allison said, in an uncomfortable manner.

Willie drank from his beer and laughed. A compassionate look came over Willie's face. My cousin was a guest and he didn't want to hurt his feelings. "Heritage not hate," Willie said, still laughing. "A good share of this country's historians are Southern and they and other historians like to write about the brave men who fought and died for the noble cause of State Rights, an action they would call treason by any other population. Sedition—that's an ugly word—but that's the word that describes the heritage of the South, come on man, you could easily satisfy these people with some whites only water fountains."

Allison took a sip from his beer, but he was clearly uncomfortable. He felt Willie was calling black South Carolinians to account for their inability to check the excesses of white South Carolinians. This wasn't how I had envisioned this night, I was hoping Sleepy Willie would have gone light on my cousin and talked about his many dissatisfaction with the quality of neck bones, or something . . . anything else.

"When I was a boy in South Carolina," Willie continued, " the ruling white classes used things like Whites Only water fountains to elevate poor whites and ignorant whites and insecure whites, above black people—in their minds. This is the tool the white ruling class used to stay on top of society—black and white. They handicapped white people with a false sense of superiority to keep them from uniting with black people to seize a proper share of political and economic power. The white ruling class knows that political and economic power is what it is all about, but the racially handicapped white person is satisfied with the illusion of white superiority."

"That's cold manipulation," I said.

"Ol' Capt'n Dan happy as a lark to supply them with plenty white superiority in the form of Whites Only water fountains long as the money and the power stays in the big house on the hill," Willie sang."

"That's what they're doing with the Confederate flag," Allison said, his eyes wide open. They are using the Confederate flag to satisfy some white people's need to be off to themselves."

"Whites only water fountains, the flag, the back of the bus," Willie said, "it's all the same, something to make Trailer Park Sue and Billy Bob feel that they are better because they've got something that is for whites only."

"When will it end?" I asked.

"It won't be long now," Willie said. "This is the last sizable generation of whites with the power to impose their will. This is also the last generation of whites with a need for this kind of thing. And the last generation of African Americans that will tolerate it."

"I don't know how we got off onto this thing," I said.

"Oh, I don't mind," Allison said. "For a man who hasn't been there in years, Willie knows the South."

"You bet I know the South. I lived there at a time when the harshness of the whites only South was branded into your very soul."

"I don't care about your knowledge of the South." I said, "I brought my cousin here for a good time, not conversation that insults where he lives."

"What you want to talk about?" Willie said to Allison.

"Oh, it don't matter much," Allison replied, "Ecaroh told me you like blues music."

"You can't be from the South and not have an appreciation for the blues," Willie said, "but that's the same conversation we just had."

HUSBAND CARE CENTER

This was a dark and melancholy sky that hung above the South Bronx as I walked up the Grand Concourse to the Two Cousins Bar on167th. Street. It looked like it would rain at any minute and the streets were empty. Summer in the Bronx is wall to wall people in the streets. All of the streets. Winter is catch as catch can. This dark and threatening winter day was the kind that the Don Juan's of the South Bronx speak fondly of as "lay— up time." The children are in school or at the arcades, or, if need be, down in the hallway, while the Don Juan's do their thing. For me, it was the kind of day conducive to good conversation with my buddy Sleepy Willie over a tall brandy. I turned the corner and walked down the hill.

". . . They could be run like child care centers," I heard Willie say as I entered the bar. Rosa, the barmaid was seated at Willie's table. It was still early and they were the only ones in the bar. "And maybe the government should help to fund them."

"Government fund what?" I asked as I pulled my chair out.

"Ecaroh, God, am I glad to see you," Rosa, said. "I've got stock to put up and this old man won't let me do my work. Now that you're here, you can keep him company and I can earn my keep. Can I start by bringing you a beer?"

"Two," Willie said.

"Two?" Rosa asked looking at me.

"Two," I confirmed.

Rosa retreated behind the bar and returned with two beers.
"What's this you got the government funding now?" I asked curious to hear what had caused Rosa to flee.

"We were talking about the many women we both know who go to work everyday while their man or husband is free to gallivant about chasing skirt tails all day long."

"And you, of course, came up with a government funded remedy? What would the government be funding?"

"A place for working women to leave their lazy finagling husbands while they're out earning a living. Any woman who work hard to support herself, a child or two, and a jobless man, deserves, at the very least, that he be monogamous."

"And you would have the government get involved in funding monogamy."

"Hey," Willie shot back, "the government fund all kinds of things. Lots of them, useless as tits on a boar. So why not some family orientated program? If I had my say about where my tax dollars went, this would be one of the things that would be way up on the list."

"Willie, I still don't know what you're talking about, but that aside, what would be at the top of your list?"

"Children," Willie answered. "I want my tax dollars spent making the lives of children better. Now I know that you're surprised, you thought I was going to say old folks. But, you see, in a lot of ways, when you better the lives of children, you better the lives of old folks."

"Well I am surprised, and I did think that you would say the government should spend more money on your group; either old folks, or black folks, or retired folks, or old, black, retired folks. Every time I think I have you figured out, you fool me. Willie, it's good to see you put the children ahead of yourself, and even this mysterious plan you want the government to fund. Man I am touched by your generosity."

"Before you came in," Willie said, "Rosa was telling me about Gwen Maxwell, and the stuff she put up with."

"I don't know her."

"She's not in here often. But you do know Danny, her husband."

"Danny? I can't place the face. Willie, I don't know half the people you know from this bar."

"He's a tall light skin dude. He is usually with that boy Ramrod and his brother Tencent."

"Oh, yeah, I know that group. They're known as the fox-hounds."

"Fox-hounds," Willie said with disgust, "if I were a woman married to any one of them, he would be known as the dead dog. Gwen is a sweet young lady who deserves better than Danny. That girl gets up every morning, feed her children and ready them for school, then go to work for eight hours. She has to pay rent and the other bills, clean house, cook the meals, and all her husband does is run the streets after those welfare gals."

"Willie, how do you get to know all this about these people? Man, you might be in need of a hobby—it will keep you out of other people's business."

"I'm in the street all the time. I see it happening all around me, it's unavoidable. Beside, I just told you that Rosa was filling me in on the details. That Negro has got some nerves, he's took to bedding a gal who lives in the same building as his family—top that. I say the government ought to stop wasting millions on dumb research and put some money into the creation of husband care centers."

"What? Husband-care-centers? Willie, now I know you've flipped. Rosa, are you a part of this—this lunacy?"

"No con prendi?" Rosa sang. "I have work to do. No time for gossip. Please I'm very busy."

"They would be just like the day care centers for children," Willie said, "women would leave their irresponsible out of work men there in the mornings, and pick them up after work in the evenings. The centers would have daylong classes for the men. Positive things like how to get through a job interview, the responsibilities of fatherhood, that kind of stuff to fill the day. This would give them less lay-up time and keep them out of trouble while their wives are out earning a living."

"Willie, I'm never surprised at your hair brain schemes, I thought I'd heard it all, but this is the most outrageous thing I have ever heard come from your mouth. Government funded day care centers for husbands. What a laugh."

"This is a time for innovative and unorthodox solutions," Willie said. "We've got to do whatever it takes to preserve the black family unit."

"Willie, please don't tell this to any one else, they'll call the wagon for you."

"Rosa," Willie called out, "bring two more beers."

"Come get them," Rosa hollered back, "I don't think I want to hear what you're saying."

FILTHY MCNASTY

Awhite homeless guy who calls himself filthy McNasty and hangs around our neighborhood came into the bar last Friday. He walked over to our table and sat down. Sleepy Willie leaned over his beer and looked McNasty in the eyes. "May we help you?" Willie sneered.

"Yeah," McNasty said. "It's hot. Buy me a beer."

"What!" Willie shot back. "Buy you a beer? Why mama-farmer you could have been president and you've got the nerve to ask me to buy you a beer?"

Filthy McNasty didn't seem the least bit phased by Willie's harsh declaration of McNasty's failure. He smiled a yellow tooth smile and folded his arms in the defiant way of a Hip-Hop Rapper. McNasty wore a Yankee's cap with the peak turned backwards, baggy denim pants, an over sized blue and yellow shirt, and sneakers with blinking lights in the heels. As bums go in New York City, McNasty is kind of old, maybe even Willie's age. He is old enough to be a genuine bum and not one of those synthetic ones created by the mean spirited politics of the eighties and nineties.

"I'll tell you what," McNasty said. I'll trade you a riddle for a beer. If you answer it correctly I'll work for you for a day, if not, you buy me a beer."

"Get lost," Willie said.

"If it takes five men an hour to dig a hole," McNasty went on, "how many men would it take to dig half a hole?"

Willie and I looked at each other. You call this a riddle our eyes laughed. Willie looked off towards the television at the curve end of the bar.

"I don't play games," Willie said. "Nor am I interested in riddles. Get lost."

I didn't know what to make of this, but I was kind of interested and I couldn't resist showing how bright I was.

"Two and a half." I said

"What did you say?" McNasty asked.

Willie shook his head and looked disappointed with me for participating.

"Oh no you didn't," Willie said.

"What was your answer?" McNasty repeated.

"Two and a half," I said. "If it takes five men an hour to dig a hole, it would take two and a half men to dig a half hole in the same time."

McNasty licked his lips and began to laugh. He clearly had a cold beer on his mind. He repeated my answer slowly. "Two . . . and . . . a . . . half."

"Well what's the answer?" I asked.

"There ain't no such thing as half a hole." McNasty said triumphantly. "All holes are whole holes. You can't dig half a hole. A hundred men can't dig half a hole in a hundred years. All holes are whole holes, from the tiniest holes to crater size holes. You have never seen a half a hole. Every hole you ever seen was a whole hole."

McNasty lambasted us (I say us, although Willie was not a welling participant in this experiment).

"I'm looking at some kind of hole now," Sleepy Willie said, "and it rhymes with half." His eyes steel cold and locked into mine.

"I'll take that beer now," McNasty said.

"That's the only way you'll get it," Willie said. "Just what do you want with us boy. Who do you think you are?"

"Filthy McNasty. I want my beer."

Willie looked seriously dangerous—fighting mad. So I ordered three beers and mumbled under my breath something about half a hole. After all, a scam's a scam and I had been scammed. As the beers were served McNasty began to talk as Willie looked off to the television.

"I'm the original beatnik and although I get your point about how I could have been president, being white and all, I ain't never wanted to be the president. As I've said my name is Filthy McNasty. I was down when 52nd street was 52nd street. I read Jack Kerouac, and Leroi Jones, and listened to Bird. I took my name from a bebop tune I heard Horace Silver wail. I ran the streets of Harlem, New York—heard Langston read at the 'Y,' danced to Fats Greene at the Renee. I was—and is—what Norman Mailer called the 'white Negro.' I didn't want any parts of the system. I didn't want to be a part of the game that was going down. I learned early that the system was loaded and I couldn't unload it. So I became a member of the counter-culture; the beat generation. Downbeat magazine was our bible. Parker and Monk and Diz were our deity. Miles and 'Trane and Cannonball were icons of the deity. Charley Minus was the Pope. Silver and Blakey and Timmons were high priests. Sonny Rollins, Dexter Gordon, and Max Roach preached our sermons.

"We weren't out to change the world by changing the world, we wanted to change the world by changing ourselves. We were the first generation threatened by the atomic bomb and an end to civilization. Our rejection of mainstream values made it possible for something new to win consideration. I once had a job and a woman and a normal lifestyle and I loved it. I was an editor and worked for many counter-culture publishers. My last job ended in 1968, or, maybe '69. The woman left in 1969, or maybe '70. I don't hurt anybody and try to make myself helpful to the people of my community. Now I know that you didn't ask for all of that, but I wanted to answer your question. I'm Filthy McNasty and I ain't never wanted to be president."

McNasty drank the last of his beer. I was speechless and even Willie seemed moved by what we had heard.

"I truly appreciate this beer on this hot day," McNasty said as he rose to leave.

Willie looked at McNasty then made a motion with his head for McNasty to sit.

"Rose," Willie called out, "bring this man a beer."

WHO GIVES THE GOVERNMENT

THE RIGHT

There he was big as day, a fellow who knows he wasn't allowed in the bar. As I understood it, he wasn't allowed in the bar because he never spent any money and his behavior distracted other patrons from their usual drinking patterns. He was known in the bar as a former crack-head. Permanent Underclass has said that he was long off the stuff and I believe him, so it does not bother me to talk with him. He was sitting at the table where Sleepy Willie and I usually sit.

"Yo Homeboy, what it is?" Permanent Underclass greeted me as I sat down.

"Hey Underclass. How are you doing buddy?"

"U'm in the groove twenty-four-seven and staying clean. You know, doing what I gotta do. You see where u'm coming from Homeboy?"

"I hear you," I said. "Can I buy you a beer?"

"Yo, my man," Permanent Underclass said and we bumped fist twice. "That would be with it, Home. Keep them mammy jammies off my case 'bout me not buying drinks in this hole in the wall."

"Well it is a business with the express purpose of making money. You do respect that, don't you?"

"And that gives them the right?"

"They're trying to make a living Underclass, you have to understand that."

"Yeah, but um trying to live. All I want to know is who gives them the right."

"Yo Homeboy, like I see where you're coming from, but all I want to know is who give them the right. Who give all these people the right to pull my strings?"

I ordered two beers. "I'll bet you're talking about something else?' I said.

"No I ain't talking 'bout nothin' else Um in a thing now where I'd like to know where everybody get there power from. Like who gives doctors the right to charge too much for treatment? Who? Who gives cops the right to shoot people down in the streets? Who? Who gives the mayor the right to spent all the tax money on white people? Who? Who gives the government the right to do whatever it wants to do? Who?'

"The right to do what—govern?" I asked.

"Yeah, word, homeboy. You a college Joe, run that down to me."

"Our government get their power to govern from the people. In this country we elect people to rule us.'

"Yo, wait a minute Homey. Am I a people?"

"Of course, underclass, you're a person."

"Word—um a person. Well I didn't elect nobody to dis me with all that funny shit they be running."

"Do you vote?" I asked.

"No. That's just a game Homeboy. They hoodwink crazy people with that voting game—telling them that their votes count. Count for what? People who get down with that voting shit need to have their heads examined."

"No Permanent underclass, it's just the other way around. People who don't vote and then complain are the ones who need to form a line in front of the shrink's office."

"Yo, Homeboy we even have black people going to see psychiatrist now. You know the world is messed up when black Americans have to be treated by shrinks."

"What makes you say that?" I asked. "We sometimes get

over burdened with the weight of problems the world deals us."

"Problems like what?" Permanent Underclass asked.

" We're just like everybody else. We have the same problems everybody else have and then some. Family problems, career problems, health problems, oh there are a host of things that can mess up our heads in this modern society."

"Problems of the modern world. Yo' Homeboy if ever there was something that would mess up a man's head, I mean just flip a mammy jammy out, it was slavery. Word. There ain't shit in this modern world that can compare to that and I ain't never heard of a slave having a shrink. Have you?"

"Underclass, the field of psychiatric study wasn't developed until after slavery."

"So Homeboy, you telling me that people didn't go crazy until there was psychiatrist to tell them they was crazy?"

"No, I don't mean that at all. There were always people with psychological problems, but there were no scientific treatments until early in the twentieth century."

"Okay Homey," Permanent Understand said, "if some black people are stressed out from modern day problems, what do you think was the affects of slavery on the slave's mental well being? I mean could a slave wake up one morning and say to himself, 'I just can't cope with this slavery shit today I think um gonna go talk to my shrink,' hell no. The Negro slave had to be mentally stronger then his so-called master. And slaves had to have minds superior to these stressed out modern black folks, to survive what they did what you think Home boy?"

"Underclass, you've taken me around as many corners as Sleepy Willie would have in a conversation and I wonder what gives you the right? Just the same, I think you're on to something. Our slave ancestors developed mechanism and institutions that gave them the endurance to survive even the brutality of slavery without the help of Sigmund Freud. Our music and our church made a direct connection with God and gave us mental stability. And now as we assimilate more and more into the main-stream culture, we lose touch with the mechanisms and institutions that saved our ancestors from mental disorder. I think it was a matter of faith then. Today we need more than faith, today, we need to act on our faith."

Turk, a long time patron on the Two cousin's bar walked over to our table. He looked down at us and pointed to Permanent Underclass as he shouted out to Rosa, the barmaid, "what's this piece of shit doing in my watering hole?" Then looking at me he said, "You talk to anything don't you?"

"How you doing Turk?" I said. "Yes."

"What I want to know," Permanent Underclass said as Turk walked away, "is where does he get the right?"

JUST FOLLOW THE TRACKS

I jumped off the "CC" train at 145th street just in time to dash across the platform and squirm into the closing doors of the last "D" train making local stops up the Grand Concourse in the Bronx. I was going two stops to 161st street. The train was jammed packed and I leaned uncomfortably against the door. The train made a sluggish lunge ahead that threw people on each other. Anything can happen on a New York City subway train. I felt someone pinch my arm as the train roared forward.

"Where you headed man?" Sleepy Willie asked.

"Hey Willie, what a surprise to see you on the train. What in the world made you leave the Bronx?"

"I had to take care some business downtown," Willie murmured as thought to say he didn't want to talk about it.

"Yeah, well, I'm on my way home to a hot shower and a hot meal. It's been a long day for me."

"I'm going home too," Willie said, "right after I stop by the bar for a cold one. You want to join me?"

"I don't think so man, I'll catch you on the weekend. Hey, did you read in the papers about that young boy who operated a passenger train all the way out to Brooklyn and back up to 207th street and operated so well the passengers couldn't tell the difference," I asked Willie changing the subject from the bar.

"I did," Willie said, taking the bait, "that was some story. I saw it on the late news last night and again this morning. The boy is a 16-year-old high school student. That young man took a trainload of people out into rush hour service and the Transit Authority didn't know a thing about it for hours."

"That's what they say," I said. They had to know something. Trains leave the terminal station at an assigned time. Where was the Train Operator who was assigned to that run? Wasn't he interested in knowing who got on his train before he did and took off with it? Believe me Willie, somebody knew something."

"It was an 'A' express train from up in Washington Heights. You know how fast those motormen drive the expresses. That boy had to be some good."

"Willie, you don't drive trains, you operate trains. The people who operate trains are call Train Operators."

"Drive, operate," Willie said, "what's the difference, all you got to do is follow the tracks. Besides, the boy said that a motorman trained him. He had been riding the train with this motorman and the motorman showed him how to drive the train."

"I'm sure the boy didn't use the terms drive or motorman," I said.

"The boy said he was trained by a motorman," Willie repeated. They found out that the boy had been riding with this motorman for months operating his train in passenger service. Then when the motorman thought the boy was good enough; he would sit outside the train cab and read the newspaper while the boy did his job. People in that first car who saw the two of them must have thought that one of them was a new trainee."

"That Train Operator, if they know who he is, is in bad trouble. I'm talking out—in the streets. His job is gone."

"I don't think they should fire him for teaching someone something, Willie said. In the news, they said that the motorman was on vacation the day this happened. There's no indication that the motorman encouraged the boy to steal the train. They can't blame him for that, only for teaching the boy to, as you put it, to operate the train. Now that doesn't sound that bad does it? Plus, they say, the boy's train was on time and that he made smooth station stops."

"I don't know how you could say that Willie, that boy made lots of trouble for himself, for the Train Operator he says trained him, for the Train Operator who should have been on that train, for the dispatcher in the control office where the boy signed on at, and for the M.T.A. in general. I mean it looks really bad for the M.T.A. that the system is so loose that someone can walk in off the streets, get on a train and endanger the lives of hundreds of people."

"I still think firing the motorman would be going too far," Willie said.

"Look there are train buffs all over the system," I said. "They ride the train lines from end to end; they know almost everything there is to know about trains and the subway system. This kid is obliviously a train buff who took his fascination too far."

"Or maybe he took Duke Ellington literally," Willie said smiling, "he took the 'A' train through Harlem."

"And got people fired," I added.

"If it's true like the boy says, the motorman taught him how to drive a train, not how to cut cocaine or cook crack. Learning to drive a train is a positive thing. More of us should be teaching our youth to do our jobs. *Each one teach one*, reads a sign in The Liberation book store on Lenox Avenue in Harlem."

"That's true, but there are ways to go about teaching our youth," I said. "We're got to do it within the system, especially with a job that could endanger people's lives."

"Every person who can teach a young black boy something positive," Willie said, "ought to get busy. We ought to be giving out metals to people for training black boys to catch crooks, build houses, buy and sell stock, mend broken bones, design computer systems, head governments, write, operate businesses, farm, teach, preach, and yes, operate trains."

Our train pulled into the 155th station making a hard stop that threw people around. I looked at Willie.

"I got on this train at West 4th Street, eight station ago," Willie said, "and who ever is driving this train ain't made a smooth stop yet. From what was said about that young boy's operation, we could be sure that's not him driving this train. Instead of making a big fuss, the M.T.A. should hire that youth to train this operator how to make smooth stops."

The train took off again, headed now towards that stretch of tunnel that lay under the Harlem River between Manhattan and the South Bronx.

96-MUNG

N.Y.P.D. BLUES

I was walking past a popular Spanish/America restaurant on the Grand Concourse when I ran into my young friend Permanent Underclass. He was going in to get something to eat and invited me along. Permanent Underclass was animated and seemed excited. We sat down at a table with white oilcloth. It was dinnertime and the restaurant was crowded. A pretty girl came to our table right off to get our order. Permanent Underclass ordered chicken and rice. I ordered a bowl of seafood soup.

"Where you coming from Ecaroh?" Permanent Underclass asked.

"Home," I answered, "I'm on my way to meet with Sleepy Willie. What's going on with you my man, how are you?"

"I just got back uptown. I was downtown at 1 Police Plaza kicking it with the protest rally against police brutality. They had a pretty good turn out, but where were you?"

"I didn't know there was a rally today," I said, "I've been busy working. Things are good and hectic on my job."

"You do know about the recent police shootings?" Underclass asked.

"Yeah, I know about them. I saw the reports on the news. I just didn't follow up on them. It's really too depressing."

"Like that's the problem," Underclass said. "Black people too busy going about their daily lives to notice important things going on in the black community. And nobody knows nothing until something happens to their family. When one of them cracker cops shoots some one from your family then you'll take time to know what's going on."

"I guess I deserve that."

"I don't mean just you," Underclass said, "I was running that down in a generic way. Every black family in this city should have had somebody down there today. Homey we are in a life or death struggle to survive. The police are gunning us down in the streets and there ain't nothing to stop them yet."

"Well if everyone gets involved like you say, then the police commissioner and the mayor will see how serious the situation is and then they will have to act. I promise you I will be at the next protest rally."

"The police commissioner and the mayor are the clean-up men. It's their job to sweep the shit under the rug. There will be no justice from them. They are the reason cops in this town feel safe gunning down black and Hispanic people. Don't be for Reverend 911 killer cops go unnoticed.

"Oh, I see," I said, "then public opinion is the purpose of the protest rally. The leaders of the rallies want to use public outrage to make the mayor and commissioner do the right thing."

The young lady brought our food with butter and Cuban bread. Underclass asked her to bring us two glasses of water and started to butter a piece of bread.

"Look Ecaroh, you my dog. You been in this city longer than me 'cause you older than I am, and you know what's going on. But let me remind you of some things you may have forgotten. You old enough to remember when some white people lived in city housing projects right?

"Yeah, I am, but you're not. That was back in the fifties."

"What happened to them?'

"They moved out to the suburbs."

"You know that. And, in time, they developed the view that the city is some kind of concentration camp. Then they passed that belief on to their children. Homey, it's those children and the children of those children of white people who fled to the suburbs in the fifties who are now patrolling New York City. Their job is to protect white suburbanites on their daily trips into the city to make a living, and when they come to Yankee Stadium and Madison Square Garden. Simple as that."

"With all that's been happening, what you say seems exactly right. Over the last twenty years the cops in this town has gotten away with killing a lot of black and Hispanic people with impunity. Back in the fifties and sixties the black community would respond with what was called riots. The legal structure looked the other way as it does today, but at lease there was some kind of reaction from us. I just can't figure how this could still be happening today."

"Let me run it to you." Underclass said as he ate. "Them white boys they hire as cops come out of them lilly white suburban high schools with that attitude I told you about and they got two career courses to choose from. They can join the mob or N.Y.P.D. Blue. Here's how they see it, in the mob you have to work your ass off. Wise guys spend long days and nights plotting and scheming and carrying out their felonies. Plus the pay in the mob ain't that great at entry level and they have to go to jail a time or three to get ahead. Wise Guys survive on the authority of fear, but their authority is only known among themselves and the people they deal with. A Wise Guy could walk down the street and we wouldn't know him from Archie Bunker. Then there is this fact; mob work is probably the most dangerous work you can do in New York City. Almost as dangerous as being a young black man and certainly lots more dangerous then being a policeman. These young white boys weigh this against joining the police. The starting pay for a cop for an eight-hour day is enough to handle a mortgage outside of the city. And instead of going to jail they get to send people to jail. Plus they get to kill people in the Bronx. Now scope this out Homey, for the ones cool with it, they still can work for the mob on the side. Shit, the choice is clear there. The New York City Police department provides better opportunity than the mob for a white boy from the suburbs. They get to do lots of the same shit, make good money and kill people. Beat that."

"Underclass, I really feel bad about not being at that rally. There has got to be some public outrage expressed. It's a sorry state of affairs and if we don't do it, who will?

"It may be time to get funky with it," Underclass said. "Do you remember years back, when they shot gunned an old black woman to death saying that they just wanted to evict her from her apartment?"

"Yeah, I'll never forget it. That was a particularly barbaric and brutal slaying."

"Now can you get real with this as an explanation; they called the police on a lady because she is supposed to be behind on her rent and refuses to vacate her place. The Precinct Commander sensing the danger of an aging black woman sent in a S.W.A.T. team. They go to the woman's apartment ram her door down and when she appears at the door frighten and bewildered with a kitchen knife in her hand, they shot gunned her to death. Man; pinch me when this shit gets real."

"I find this difficult to talk about. It makes me raging mad." I said.

"Lemme hip you to this," Underclass said. "Picture this being a white woman in one of those old black and white movies from the forties. She is sitting at her kitchen table looking in her empty sugar bowl where she keeps the rent money. 'Oh my, there isn't a cent left for rent,' she says as the camera pan in on the eviction notice she holds in her hand. The screen goes black for a second. In the next scene a black telephone is ringing on a large wooden desk. A hand lifts the phone and from a wide camera shot we see that it's the Precinct Captain played by Pat O'Brian. In the next scene, O'Brian's got all the cops together and he's talking to them. 'It's like this you mugs, this lady is behind on her rent, you see. Oh, it don't matter why, it could be your ma or mine. The point is we gotta do something, so I'm gonna ask all you flat foots to give what you can.' The camera pans in on O'Brian holding his hat out and all the cops gladly forking out the bucks. In the next scene, the old lady is holding the money near her heart and thanking the boys for their generosity. Another good deed by the New York City Police Department. Dog, they don't make those kind of movies any more because they're no longer reality based."

"I remember the whole affair," I said. "Those cops went on trial right here in the Bronx and was exonerated by a judge. They had the option not to tried by a jury of their peers and they grabbed that up. They knew that in the Bronx a jury of their peers would have given them justice."

"Word." Underclass said. "It's not just the racist killer cops we're up against, but also the justice system that lets them get away with murder. Homie, its time. We've got to strike back," Underclass said pounding his hand on the table.

"What do you mean by that?" I asked, sensing the recklessness of frustration entering our conversation."

"It is time to end this slaughter by any mean necessary. An eye for an eye. They do one of ours; we do one of theirs."

"Nobody wins that one," I said, "especially not us. We need to get political. We need to elect a mayor and a city council that will adopt measures that will make every cop live in the city. You have to live in the city to become its mayor; no one should be able to hold a police job unless they live in one of the five boroughs. And, we need to get more minorities on the police force. That's a tall order, but there is where we need to start."

"In the mean time," Underclass replied, "somebody need to organize a small cadre of avengers to let them know that no unclean killing will go unchallenged. What you're talking about will take a century. You know how many of us they will have killed by then? Besides that, how's your program gonna work, when up-right citizens like you don't get involved?" Underclass pushed his plate away in discuss.

I spooned up the last shrimp from the soup bowl and gave

Underclass a look that conceded his point. I found it trouble-some that Permanent Underclass, an ex-crack head, street rogue, was engaging in a responsible civic manner while I, an outwardly ideal citizen, with a responsible position, had become a part of the problem. I wondered how many people there are like me, middle class, isolated, and aloof? How much clout could we bring to the fight against police brutality? Why hadn't the black middle class applied its prestige and influence to the problem? Could it be that we feared that when it comes to the question of police brutality, we would find that we have neither prestige nor influ-ence? After all, even a black mayor was unable to control the excesses of the N.Y.P.D. The thought tied my stomach in a knot.

"You're absolutely right man," I said, finally able to look Underclass in his eyes, "too many people in the black middle class have been silent and inactive for far too long. I tell you what I'm going to do; I'm going to call some friends and orga-nized a group to aid the National Action Network in any way we can. I promise you man, I won't miss another protest against police brutality."

" I hear that. But I want you to know that all-close eyes ain't sleep and all good-byes ain't gone. This Saturday we are going to DC to protest in front of the Justice Department, while our lead-ers try to get the Attorney General to investigate the New York Police Department. Why don't you and your group join us? The bus ride is free."

"Saturday, I really don't know," I said already sliding back from my just stated commitment. Permanent Underclass fired a worn look of disgust my way that jarred me back to my commitment.

"I'm going to make it man. What time and where are the buses leaving from?"

"We are loading up in front of the Apollo Theater at seven in the morning."

"I'll see you there and I'm going to tell Sleepy Willie about it. It will be interesting to see if he will leave the South Bronx."

"Mr. Walker is an old man," Underclass said, "but he's a down dude from the old school."

After paying our bills, we walked out of the restaurant together. Underclass was on his way to a meeting and I to the Two Cousins bar to meet with Sleepy Willie.

"Over here, Ecaroh," Willie shouted out as I entered the bar. He was seated at an unusual table near the rear of the room. It is only when both of us get there late that we lose our table by the window.

"How was your day?" I asked as I sat down.

"Exciting and productive," Willie said a pleased smile on his face. "I got back up-town late after spending most of the day at 1 Police Plaza protesting Police Brutality. I'll tell you all about that in a minute, but first let me tell you where you and I are going Saturday."

"Saturday?" I said.

"Yeah, Saturday. Saturday, we're taking the protest to Washington DC."

"My maaaan," I said.

EL' BARRIO RESARIO

"We are all just very lucky," Sleepy Willie said, "the city is lucky, The Bronx is lucky, we're all just lucky. This could have caused bloodshed all over the city. The people are disgusted and mad as hell. But the word is he wants the people to wait for justice. We are lucky that they do what he asked."

His name is Raymond Rosario. He is a first generation Puerto Rican American. His grand father brought his family to New York City in 1950. The family finally settled in the Amsterdam Housing Projects, where Raymond's father grew up. Raymond was born there in 1961 and grew up in the same neighborhood as his father. The same neighborhood Sleepy Willie haunted many years earlier. In fact Willie knew his grand father and his father, but didn't meet Raymond until they started hanging around the same bar in the South Bronx.

After two years of college, Raymond joined the New York City Police Department in 1982. A few years later he married and settled in an apartment on the Grand Concourse across from the courthouse. Just two blocks from his beloved Yankees. Raymond has been a detective for many years now. Everybody in the South Bronx knows he is a cop, but he is also a Bronx icon. This man is positively revered. This is because of the admirable way he conducts his personal life and his official life. And because of all the productive things he's done for the community over the years. He organizes winter and summer sports for the community's youth. He counsels kids in trouble as well as kids attending the Bronx High School of Science. When there is a problem, he is the man to call. He has gone to bat for youths wronged by other cops and he's tried to explain the roll of the police to the community. He is a successful street-wise guy, who talks, walks, and processes the deportment of his neighbors. And he doesn't take any crap from anyone. Raymond Rosario is loved by everyone and is known affectionately by everyone as El' Barrio Resario, the de facto mayor of the South Bronx. El' Barrio Resario, the man. He is well connected to high authorities in the Bronx and to the street underworld and is often the bridge between the two. All this, and a loving husband to a wife who is a high school principal and father of two teenage girls, one of whom is in college. Talk about a full plate.

A few weeks ago while Willie and I sat in the Two Cousins Bar drinking beer and talking. El' Barrio Resario walked in and after much hand shaking, back patting and the dignitary treatment he made it to our table. He is a brown skin tall guy. Playing paddleball keeps his body thin and in shape. A thick black moustache adorns his warm friendly face.

"What's happening Homeboy," El Barrio greeted Sleepy Willie, referring to their old neighborhood connection. "Ecaroh Lee, my man," he greeted me as cheerfully as he had Willie.

"Sit down," Willie ordered. "Let me buy you a beer," said the man who until this point had been drinking on my tab.

El Barrio Resario sat down, "I'll have one," he said, as Willie and I welcomed him simultaneously, "but I don't have much time."

"Man, how are you doing?" Willie asked. "It's been months since I've seen you."

"I'm doing fine. Fit as a fiddle as they say out west," El Barrios said. "I just stay too busy and it's getting hard for me to keep up with it all. Always something that needs doing, like yesterday. Now summer is coming and I've got to get my baseball league and my basketball league staffed and geared up. I can't sit and drink beer half the day like some people."

"Bring this man a beer," Willie shouted to Rosa, the barmaid.
"I was hoping I was going to find you here Ecaroh."
"Oh yeah, what's up?"
"I need basketball referees. I'm short of referees for the summers games. You refereed for me a few summers ago and you did a great job, but then you cut me loose. What you doing this summer man?"
"I don't know. We haven't planned our vacation date yet. I know we are going to spend a week in South Carolina some time during the summer, but nothing is certain yet."
"Well all the games are going to be played on Sundays. Only thing is there will be some Sundays when you'll have to referee two or three games. But, when you take your vacation, that's fine, I'll get a replacement for that Sunday. What you say man, come on sign up with me. With all the shit that's been going on in this city, this is going to be a troublesome summer. Let's work to keep our kids busy and out of trouble."
I didn't answer, but I knew he had me.
" Willie, my dad tells me all the time about a man name Sam Benerson down in the Amsterdam projects. He use to organize bus-rides and tournaments in the sixties. You knew him?
"Champagne Shorty, is what some of us called him, but most people called him Baron" Willie said. "He was a smart classy guy, with big ideas and a civic mind, something like yourself. He was a man who could pull the community together and get everybody involved for the betterment of the community."
"Well just like he couldn't do it all by himself, neither can I. So what you say Ecaroh?"
"Alright, you got me," I said as the barmaid brought three beers and told us that someone at the bar had paid for them all in honor of the presence of El' Barrio Resario.
El' Barrio Resario stood up from the table, hoist his bottle of beer above his head and said, "for the boys up state," then took a drink before he sat down. "I want to say thank you, Ecaroh."

Then he took a form from his pocket and put it on the table before me. "Fill this out," he directed.

"Don't you look at me," Willie said, "I'm too old to be running around in that hot summer sun."

"I'll give you that," El' Barrio said, "but I'll find a way for you to volunteer your support. I'm not going to let anybody get away this coming summer. We are going to need all the volunteers we can get. Tensions are running high after all the police shooting over the last year or so and we are all going to do what we can to keep things cool. You know Willie, we'll need score keepers."

"I can do that," Willie said.

That was the last time we saw El' Barrio before the tragedy. It happened last Friday evening. The bar was crowded with people just back uptown from work. Willie and I sat at our table by the window when a guy came rushing into the bar with horror on his face. He was beating his chest and shouting incoherently. Some people who knew the guy went over to calm him down and find out what happened. They were shouts of "What, what?"

"What happened?" Willie asked the people at a table closer to the fellow than we were.

"El' Barrio just got wasted," someone at the table replied. The bar felled silent. Rosa, the barmaid handed the fellow a drink and he gulped it down before he started to tell what he knew in a distraught manner.

"It, it jus, it just happened. Maybe half-hour or so ago. I heard the shots. I was walking up the Concourse by the park. I turned around towards the sound, but I didn't see anything. The shots came from the other side of the park. I was gonna keep on walking, but I saw people from the courthouse running to that section of park over by the flower shop. The police were all over the place telling people to move on. By the time I got to where I could see something they had the whole area roped off. People were moving around trying to see what had happened, but the police kept everyone back. Someone said something about a holdup at the flower shop that two white guys outside the flower

shop shot El' Barrio. Two EMS trucks drove off with police es-
corts."

"Let's go." someone in the bar shouted. Willie grabbed my
arm and spoke to me with his eyes. In little time, the mob fled the
bar. Everyone was gone except for Rosa, Willie and I.

"If this is true," Willie said, "you don't want to be there . . .
not right now. This means nothing but trouble, the same kind of
trouble El' Barrio spends so much of his time trying to prevent.
He would want us to be cool and move with caution."

We sat around for an hour feeling the anxiety of the event. A
few people returned to the bar. They were all in a dire mood.
There was much cussing and loud talk about revenge, but there
was not one clear picture of what had happened. More people
returned to the bar, but stood outside talking in agitated and
angry gestures. The only thing we learned was that El' Barrio was
indeed shot. Some said by two white policemen. Some said it was
a mob hit, others said drug barons were responsible. The rumors
sent Willie and I home to watch the evening news.

On the evening news, it was reported that El' Barrio had just
left the courthouse on police business. He had gone to the small
flower shop across the street from the park to buy flowers for his
wife's birthday. As he arrived at the flower shop, there was a
robbery in progress. A young-armed black man was backing out
of the door. El' Barrio tackled the robber knocking the gun from
the hand of the surprised young man. A scuffle took place that
ended outside on the street. El' Barrio subdued the robber pin-
ning him to the ground and took out his own gun. A crowd was
forming that attracted the attention of two white plain-clothes
police officers who had just recently completed giving testimony
at the courthouse and were approaching their car. The two officers rushed to the scene and saw a black man banishing a gun
pushing another black man up side a wall. They pulled their
guns and shouted out for the man with the gun to drop it.

Now here is where even the news account gets murky. The
officers involved have not made a statement on the advice of

union counsel. The official police account is that the man did not respond to the officer's demand. The officers, as they're trained, reacted in a split second. The officers shot fearing for the safety of the man against the wall, the crowd, and themselves. The case was being investigated by Internal Affairs office of the Police Department, and The Bronx District Attorney.

Reporters found eyewitnesses who said that the man with the gun shouted back that he was a cop. All of the witnesses said the man was reaching in his shirt for his badge, which hung on a chain around his neck when three shots rang out hitting him twice and the man against the wall once. The two men fell to the ground. One of the cops kicked the gun from the fallen cop's right hand as the two approached. The cop lay atop the robber, his left-hand gripping the badge hanging from the chain around his neck. The news report concluded with a statement from the police commissioners and the mayor calling for the community to remain calm while the investigation went on. All that we have been able to find out from that time to this night is that the officers involved in the shooting were assigned desk jobs pending the conclusion of the investigation. El'Barrio was recovering and would be coming home in a few days, and that the young robber, who had an extensive police record had several charges lodged against him, and, was himself recovering from his wound.

"So if the city's luck holds up this thing will play out in the usual manner," Willie said. "Those cops will go back to work in anonymity. The public will have forgotten the event. El' Barrio will get a few million dollars in a settlement and the city will drift on to the next shooting."

PRISON LETTERS

"I heard you got busted," I said as I sat at our table. "It's a crying shame, a man your age going to jail. Willie, just what am I going to do with you?"

"You might want to give me the Medal of Freedom after you hear my reason," Sleepy Willie said. "I was coming home from the store. The kids in the block had the water hydrant on trying to keep cool. They had been playing that cat and mouse game with the police most of the day."

"Yeah I know that game from when I was a boy," I said. "They put the water hydrant on, the police come and cut it off, they put it on, the police cut it off."

"A dozen times," Willie said. "I don't know what sparked the cops this last time; maybe the air conditioner wasn't working in their car or a wife swap gone bad, but them cats got hot under the collar. They grabbed up the tallest boy there, fifteen year old Hector Hernandaz, and roughed him up. And when the boy tried to get loose from them, they clubbed his head open. Some of the children, even young girls in bathing suits went to Hector's aid. The children were crying and shouting for the police to let Hector loose. I sensed a disaster coming on. I dropped my package running up to the cops. I grabbed the cop's arm with the club coming down on the boy again. The other cop grabbed me and flung me down in the flow of the water coming from the hydrant. Just then two other cops came on the scene. They hand cuffed the young boy and me. His head was gushing blood. They threw us in the back of their car as the crowd got bigger and louder and dangerous. I tried to talk to them. Tried to get them to take Hector to a hospital, but they turned a deft ear on me. On our way to the police station I found out that the air conditioner in their car did work."

"So you sacrificed yourself to save those children from possibly being beaten by the police. Willie you're a noble man. A noble man with a police record that will follow you the rest of your life."

"There're many noble men and woman with police records," Willie said. "I'm only following in their example. And while I was entombed in the belly of the beast I wrote you a letter. I didn't know how long I would be imprisoned so I took to pen and paper to collect my thoughts and to make sure you knew where I was. But they released me the very next morning so I never got a chance to mail the letter."

"Entombed in the belly of the beast! Willie, jail brings out the poet in you man. You should have stayed longer, say, five years, and then we would have the Prison Letters of Sleepy Willie in book form. You'd be in league with the likes of Eldridge Clever, George Jackson, Martin Luther King jr., Jean Genet, Ho Chi Minh and a large group of revolutionaries who wrote lasting literary statements while imprisoned. They proved that the body can be imprisoned, but the mind and the spirit—for strong men—that's another matter."

"You forgot to mention Gandhi," Willie said.

"I know that Gandhi went to jail many, many, times in his struggles for India's independence," I said, "but I don't know if he did much prison writing."

"That don't matter," Willie smiled triumphantly." I went to jail like Gandhi, for the cause of freedom."

"Alright."

"You want to know what's in my letters?" Willie asked.

"Why not? Let's hear how jail has inspired you."

Willie called the barmaid and told her to bring two beers to our table and to put the two beers on my tab. He looked at me to take a gauge of my attitude. Sensing that I was still interested, Willie pulled a crumpled piece of paper from his pocket and ran his fingers over it to straighten it out. The barmaid returned with the beers and Willie took a drink. Then a strange look came over his face, like no other I'd seen before.

Willie read:

> *Ecaroh Lee, my dear friend and comrade, I am an old man in the autumn of my years. I am at a stage when life should be reflective, spiritual, and unhampered. But, Ecaroh, my friend, brutality and injustice run rampant in the streets still. What is an old man to do? Close his eyes? The shape and the struggle for the future belong to the young, but I've just discovered that injustice calls us all to the struggle no matter the age. Transgressions against my fellow man are transgressions against me and with my eyes open I see that it can be no other way.*
>
> *My captors and guards tell me that it is raining out side. I could be home listening to Billie Holiday and looking out my window at the rain. Instead I hear Billie's anguish in my heart and feel cleanse from the rain of my action as I sit in a windowless jail cell that I have turned into an awakening monastery. Yes, this is my monastery where I plot my future course and chant the mantra of freedom. The longer I stay here, the clearer I see.*
>
> *I am an American. The grievances of the downtrodden are my own. I am an old man with little time left, but for whatever that time, I will be a rampart against injustice. And, if necessary, I will become a ramrod for justice. Friends and foes alike will, forever more, know me as an American of action. Yes, I intervened in the brutal beating of a youth trying to cool himself from a day of scorching sun and the scalding madness of mean city streets. For that I landed in the cooler. Ecaroh, nothing could make me prouder.*

Yours in the struggle,

William (Sleepy Willie) Walker

I took a sip from my beer. Seemed I'd heard this all once before, perhaps, in the prison letters of George Jackson. If these weren't the same words, this was surely the same tone and sentiment.

"You may have addressed this letter to me in thought, but from hearing it, it sounds like a stream of consciousness, more like you were talking to yourself." I said.

"That's it," Willie said. "It was like some things I had always felt, known, and been, had surfaced in my consciousness by the incidence. Thinking them out in a letter to you just made it easier for the feelings to be reborn in me."

"I think you've rediscover some important portions of yourself, but I hope you don't intend to become an octogenarian revolutionary. Listen to me, Sleepy Willie, the sixties are over and this is a fight for young people."

"The sixties may be over, but there is still far too much injustice," Willie said.

"You ought to be enjoying life and trying to stay out of jail. Do you know what goes on in those places?"

"Let's keep this on a high plane." Willie said.

" I must admit, though, a night in jail did you some good, made a visionary out of you. But Willie, whatever happen to the boy?"

"Hector is in the hospital with a concussion. The police dropped whatever phony charges they booked him on. His parents are filing police brutality charges against the police and a lawyer from downtown with dollar signs in his eyes have been meeting with them and with me."

"So this isn't over," I said.

"Not by a long shot," Willie said. "The struggle goes on and justice will soon be ours."

THE MAD MAN OF MORRIS

AVENUE

It was near sun down on a Friday evening. Willie and I were walking off a heavy meal we had at my house. We were taking a long route to the Two Cousin's bar on the other side of Jerome Avenue. We crossed One Hundred and Sixty First Street at Morris Avenue next to Charlie Chan's two-story home. We didn't see him immediately, but Charlie Chan was sitting on his stoop. He was dressed in his bedclothes and was eating a strawberry icy. Charlie Chan is known throughout the South Bronx as the mad man of Morris Avenue. Charlie Chan is a mentally unstable fifth generation Japanese American. Charlie is a harmless guy who suffers from delusions. Members of his family worked on the California link of the western railroad during the gold rush. His grand parents moved the family from California to New York City after being imprisoned in the internment camps during World War Two.

Ben Chan, Charlie's father, is a renowned surgeon and his mother Ruth, is a Wall Street Lawyer. They live In Yonkers. Charlie's diagnosis came before he finished high school. He suffered repeated episodes of fantasy that prevented him from separating his mirage world from reality. Charlie was institutionalized twice. He had to give up college, where he was a political science major, because of the disruptive nature of his illness. After many years of keeping Charlie at home to oversee his mental treatments, the Chans were advised to let him take control of his life. They bought him the house on Morris Avenue. They pay for a weekly visit by a mental health specialist who make sure he's talking his medications, advise him on managing his household affairs and supervise his circumstances. The Chans even pay for a housekeeper who comes once a week to clean behind the mad man of Morris Avenue.

Charlie's life isn't all that bad, I'd say. He works for as long a period as he can hold on to a job, which hasn't ever been more then a few months. He is viewed in the community as sort of an exotic pet. He amuses most people and there are many people in the community who genuinely like him. He has a Korean girlfriend, and a small circle of close friends. But everyone is a friend to Charlie Chan.

"You all are just gonna walk right on by me?" Charlie said to Willie and I as we were about to past his house. He stood up on the steps to make himself better seen. "Why you all wasn't even gonna say good evening to me."

"Hey Charlie," I answered. "Didn't see you sitting there. And good evening too."

"How about you, Mr. Willie?"

"Good evening Charlie," Willie said, as we paused in front of Charlie's gate. "We're on our way to the Two Cousin's, you want to tag along?"

"I would," Charlie said, "but I'm waiting on a phone call from the White House."

"Oh, I see," I said.

"The administration still bugging you for advice," Willie said for the same reason bait is placed on a hook. Then he rested his upper body on the gate waiting for a bite. It was clear Willie wanted to engage Charlie in conversation. "It doesn't matter who is in office Republicans or Democrats, they all got your number, uh Charlie?"

"Nothing I can't handle." Charlie nibbled around the bait. "When you've been doing this as long as I have, you get to know them all. Nothing surprises me, I just go with the flow."

"Well, Charlie," I said, as I signaled Willie with an unseen tap on his arm, "we're gonna hat on up."

"Come on in and sit on the steps with me," Charlie said, completely hooked. "I'll get us a few cold ones and when that phone call comes I'll let you all speak to the president."

An offer Willie couldn't resist reeling in. He's been offered many a beers in his lifetime, but he's never been offered a chat with a president, not even an imaginary one. Willie opened the gate before the words left Charlie's mouth and in we went. Charlie threw the paper cup from the icy in a trashcan by the steps and shook our hands. He went into the house to get the beers. I shot a look of disgust towards Willie. He just smiled at me. Charlie returned and we all sat down on different steps of the stoop, Charlie up top, Willie next, and I, on the bottom level.

"So what kind of crisis are you working on for the president?" Willie asked.

"I don't talk about ongoing projects" Charlie answered. "I make it a practice to keep current work close to the vest, things just work out better this way, you know what I mean?"

"You know Sleepy Willie," I said to Charlie, apologetically, "always prying in other people's business."

" I don't mind it one bit," Charlie said. "I'd be glad to share some details from some of my past cases if you all are interested. I'll start with my work for Richard Nixon."

"Richard Nixon," Willie moaned, "you were just a little boy when Nixon resigned the presidency."

"I've been in this business for a long time now," Charlie said. I was a teenager, thirteen, I think, when I tried to save Richard Nixon's presidency, gave him the best advice I ever gave to any president since. But it may have been my age that gave Nixon's two main advisers the inside track. My advice was either not given to Nixon, or relayed in a tainted way."

"They were going to impeach Nixon," Willie said, "nothing could have saved him. They had all the details on how he masterminded the cover up of the break-in at the Democratic Headquarters in the Watergate hotel. There was nothing nobody could have done to save Nixon."

"I was going to make impeachment go away long before there was a serious call for it."

"How?" Willie wanted to know.

"If you remember, early during the Watergate investigations, Nixon's Vice President, Spiro Agnew pleaded nolo contendere to a Federal income tax charge and had to resign. This was the golden moment Nixon could have seized to rescue his doomed presidency. This was the time for a supreme Machiavellian move. All Nixon had to do was choose the right man to replace Agnew."

"And who would that have been?" Willie asked.

"Senator Edward W. Brooks of Massachusetts."

"Senator Brooks?" I asked, "Who is he?"

"He was a African American Senator," Willie informed me, "who was elected during the late sixties and served with Edward Kennedy. He was still in the senate during the Watergate period."

"But if they had the goods on Nixon, how would making Brooks Vice President save Nixon from impeachment?" I asked.

"I think Mr. Willie knows," Charlie smiled. "Oh yes, Mr. Willie knows for sure.

" I understand what he's getting at," Willie said, and the two of them burst out laughing.

"If Richard Nixon," Charlie continued, "would have nominated Senator Brooks for Vice President and gave a wink to his allies in the Senate, he still would had to pull some strings and twist some arms to get Brooks confirmed among the Republicans. But Nixon could have embarrassed the Democrats who said they were for integration into voting for Brooks. That would have been the end of the Watergate inquiry. As the Watergate investigations started heading towards a recommendation of impeachment, the realization of who was Vice President and Nixon's successor would set in and that fact itself would have shut the Watergate investigations down. Back then there was no way they would have impeached Nixon and elevate a black man to the presidency."

"I don't think that would happen today," Willie said. "But I've got to admit Charlie, that would have been an ingenious stroke. Man, you're a political genius."

"What a fantastic story," I said.

"In the late seventies I told the homeboys about the hip-hop movement," Charlie said, "it's gonna be big I advised them. I use to run with the early rappers, cats like Kool Moe Dee, Grandmaster Flash, Kurtis Blow, and the Sugarhill Gang, and Afrika Bambaataa. The emergence of graffiti art, break dancing, and rap was the foundation for the grass-roots cultural movement these dudes were creating. I warned them to claim ownership to every aspect of the movement they could and to hold on to control for as long as they could. If your thing last for more than a decade the mainstream will jump on it and goggle all of it up."

"Why?" Willie, a hip-hop opponent, wanted to know. "Why, would they want to hold on to trash music?"

"Because rap music generates billions of dollars a year," Charlie said. "Right now it's the most lucrative part of the music industry. There's lots of power in those billions, but instead of creating a power base for the creators of rap, those billions just enhanced the power of mainstream music barons. Those pioneering cats got peanuts compared to what's going down now. But, cest la vie."

"What other president have you advised," I asked.

"Gerald Ford."

"What advice did you give him?"

"To keep his head down and duck when he disembarked his helicopter and to take sure steps when he was walking off stage."

"Sound advice to a man who seemed prone to mishaps," Willie said with a little laugh. "What about Jimmy Carter?"

"Jimmy Carter used to button only the bottom button on his suit jacket. He looked like a country hick. I advised Carter to unbutton the bottom button on his suit jacket and button the top button."

"Changed his whole presidency I bet," Willie said, his sarcasm showing.

"No, his appearance," Charlie shot back, then continued to take control of the conversation. "I told Johnny Cochran to have O. J. Simpson try on the gloves that were used in the murder of his wife and her friend. I wanted it done in front of the jury, and I knew that the whole world would witness it. I told Johnny that if the glove didn't fit O.J.'s hands that would go a long way in proving O.J.'s innocence. If the glove didn't fit the jury would have to cut O.J. loose, I told Johnny.

"Who," Willie asked, "came up with 'if the glove don't fit you must acquit.'"

"That's how Johnny translated my analytical summation. And it turned out to be true. If the glove don't fit you must acquit."

"What turned out to be true?" Willie shouted.

"That the jury couldn't convict O. J. knowing that the gloves worn by the killer didn't fit him."

"Oh," Willie said, "I though you meant that it turned out to be true that O. J. was innocent."

"The jury said O.J. was not guilty," I interjected, "and while I know from serving on jury duty that that is not the same as being innocent, O.J. is a free man. Look, I've got to go." I was getting wary. The O.J. Simpson case does that to me.

"This is Friday evening," Willie said, "it's early yet. What about going to the bar? Don't tell me you aren't going to finish our chat over a cold one at Two Cousins?"

"Not tonight," I said as I dropped my empty can in the trashcan and stood up to leave, "I'm gonna pack it on in."

Just then the phone rang.

"See you later," I said to Charlie as he rose to answer the phone in the living room.

"Hold on," Charlie shouted back, "this might be the president."

"Are you leaving?" I asked Willie as I opened the gate.

"Not until I speak to the president," he said. "See you later."

96-MUNG

A NOTE FROM THE FUTURE

"Picture this, your six year old daughter comes home from school and on her face is a note written to you by her teacher with a black magic marking pen."

"On her face?" Sleepy Willie asked in disbelief. "This wasn't done because the teacher was out of paper, what does the note say?"

"The note reads 'Where are my glasses?' "

"No my man," Willie said. "The note has the wrong message. Any person who write on my child's face better write 'Where is the jaws of life,' because by the time I finish planting my foot that is what will be needed to remove it."

"Willie, I can expect that kind of reaction from you. But don't you see, then the issue would not be what the teacher did, but rather, your violence against the teacher."

"Let me tell you something," Willie said in a grim tone, "writing on a child's face is an act of violence. Any person, ah, but especially a school teacher, a person with whom you entrust your child, who commits an act of violence on a child provokes a natural reflex reaction from the parents. If you ever tried to touch the young of any animal, you would provoke a protective reflex reaction from the parents, humans aren't any different. The reflex reaction to violence against a child is violence against the perpetrator. So yeah, we would discuss the issue after that teacher was made to understand the boundary. Then I would hire a team of lawyers, maybe even the Dream Team."

"Lawyers. Willie, what are you going to do with lawyers?"

"Reinforce my point by suing everybody in sight. The teacher, the school, the School board, the Department of Education, the colleges the teacher graduated from, the teacher's mama and daddy. Man, you think that the O.J. case went on forever. When I got finish suing people and institutions there would be a up-turn on Wall Street."

"Wall Street? Please explain."

"That's right, Wall Street. Paper producing companies will be the hot stock to buy. I would raise so much cane that every school system in the country would be ordering more paper note pads for their teachers than the companies could produce. There wouldn't be a tree left standing in America, but the face writing would be stopped."

" I think I've let you go off on the deep end on this, when it's obvious you haven't heard any thing about it."

"No, this is the first I've heard of it. Don't see how that would make what I say about how I would react any less valid."

"Well maybe it doesn't, but tell me Willie, where do you think it happened?"

"Probably in some school right here in the South Bronx."

"No. It happened in your home state."

"Well it could have happened here," Willie said somewhat defensively. "But I'm not surprised that it happened in South Carolina. South Bronx, South Carolina, you attach the word South to a location and strange things happen. When I die and go to heaven I pray I don't get assigned to a section called South Heaven."

"What if you go to that other place?"

"Hell! There ain't any different parts of hell. All of hell is South."

"The teacher is white and the child is black," I said, "but the good white folks of South Carolina say that race played no part in the matter."

"Well I'll tell you one thing," Willie said, race should play no part in how people react to this act of violence against a child. Everybody should be outraged that this thing could happen in a classroom. There is no defense for this kind of violence except when it happens in South Heaven. Now tell me what is this all about?"

"It seems that this child had come to school without her eye glasses time and again. The teacher tried to impress on the mother the importance of the child having her glasses in class—to no avail, in frustration the teacher took to the magic maker and the child's face to convey her message."

"Right message, wrong medium," Willie said, "and my foot is still where it was at the beginning of this conversation. But let me tell you why I think they're so quick to rule out race as a factor. They feel that mistreatment motivated by racism will stigmatize them, where as mistreatment absent racial motivation isn't even mistreatment. So in South Carolina when a schoolteacher write on a child's face, or in the South Bronx when a policeman shoots an unarmed black teen, there is this rush to discount race as a motive, that makea everything else cool. We are at a place in America, where whites can commit wrongs against blacks and have the slate wiped clean if they can make it seem free of racial inspiration."

"So if the child was also white," I laid my ambush, "you still consider the act an act of violence."

"Of course so," Willie answered quickly.

"Well this teacher was reported to have written on the faces of several of her white students without incident. Although to be fair, reportedly, the marks on the white students faces were of a less hostile nature."

"Look," Willie said, "there is lots of paper in schools, teachers don't have to write on anyone's face—that's why they have notepads. The real point here isn't what some parents will tolerate, but how teachers are taught to teach. The other thing here is that black folks ought to point first to the crime—then racism, when it can be proven. A crime is a crime. A racially motivated crime is two crimes, the illegal act itself, and the fact the act is motivated out of racial bias. We let white perpetrators off the hook by giving them the chance to first show that a crime is not racially motivated, for them that means there was no crime. So we need to focus on the deed itself, and I'm no Johnny Cochran."

"I agree with all of that."

"If we don't," Willie said, "we will continue to receive these little notes from the future written on the faces of our children. And that's not the kind of future we want to pass on to our children."

CULTURAL COLONIALISM

"If you want to see where a nation is going, look at its culture somebody once said," Sleepy Willie said.

"Oh yeah, who?" I replied.

"I don't recall, but somebody said it."

"Then it's currency without current value." I said.

"Huh?" Willie said.

"It ain't necessarily so." I said.

"It was also said that the sun never sets on the British Empire."

"Also a currency without current value," I said. "Hong Kong was the last valuable colony the British controlled, but they had to return it to China. And the lights finally went out on the British Empire."

"And to land colonization," Willie added, "but America is colonizing the world in another manner."

"How's that?"

"By exporting its culture. That's right, cultural colonization. What's hip in America is what the rest of the world's people aspire too. American music, American television, clothes, dance, movies, speech, American mores and habits. This is the current method of colonization. No troops, no guns and blood, no political mess."

"Colonialism," I said, " is the process of militarily taking over a country, subjugating its people, then looting its natural resources. The British was the best at it. At one time they had colonized all of India, parts of China, large parts of Africa, much of the Mid-East, some islands in South America, a rock in Spain, and a little of this, and a little of that in other parts of the world. But it took lots of troops and harsh oppression to hold on to it all for as long as they did."

"All that kind of thing is just about over," Willie said. "Today's colonizers produce television programs, design fashion, and advertise on MTV. People from Russia to Nigeria, China to Peru want to be Americanized."

"So tonight's topic is the Americanization of the world," I said.

"No," Willie said. "What we'll talk about is the African-Americanization of planet earth. Listen, what's hip in American is what the world wants. But it's what's hip in black America that is hip in the broad American culture. Much of American culture is driven by what comes out of Harlem and America's other black inner-cities."

"Then America is the great melting pot," I said. "Willie, this is a concept you always said doesn't exist."

"We'll talk about that melting pot junk some other time. My point is that much of American popular culture comes from African-American popular culture. The African in America is turning white America—culturally—black. If you don't believe me look at the cultural war politics of Patrick Buchanan. The exporting of American culture is creating the African-Americanization of the world."

"Willie, do you really think that African-American culture has that great of an influence on the mainstream American culture?"

"Obviously more than you know. More than many white people besides Buchanan, would want to admit. Listen to me, much of what passes as mainstream American cultural mores today has its roots in black American culture. If only my old friend Hyman Nespitt were still here to see how much black culture whites have adopted—I hate to say stolen."

"Who is Hyman Nespitt?"

"He was a friend from my old San Juan Hill neighborhood downtown. He would understand what I'm talking about here."

"And I don't?"

"Old Satchmo," Willie said without answering me, " would have been amazed to see that 'gimme some skin' has gotten to be the 'high five'. The 'down boys' of Harlem, who Langston Hughes often wrote about must feel violated when they see even white politicians use the triple grasp hand shake, which was originated to identify one 'down boy' to another."

"Willie, it sounds to me like you are merely complaining because a few black cultural traits have made it into the mainstream."

"I's not complaining, I's explaining," Willie said somewhat derisively. "I don't care if they mimic us until they're black in the face."

"Is that a joke?"

"No. Let me tell you a little story. Back in the fifties, some of the young guys from the San Juan Hill section of mid-Manhattan, was into that heroin thing. They had to go up to one hundred and fifteenth street in Harlem to cop. The young boys from San Juan Hill were too naïve to be dealing with those slick dope dealers from Harlem. They had all kinds of swindles and scams pulled on them up in Harlem. Most of the scams were accomplished with high finesse. The boys from downtown would refer to these swindles simply as 'getting beat.' But then there were times when they would give their money to someone who would then simply disappear. Hyman Nespitt was the first one to refer to this as getting ripped off; being swindled without finesse, ripped off."

"How long ago was this Willie? The term ripped off is in the dictionary."

"This was in the fifty's," Willie said. "It's in the modern dictionary, but that's not the only place you'll find it. The term Hyman invented to describe a bad narcotic transaction is today most often used by Democratic and Republican politicians to describe each other's treatment of the American people. Ecaroh, If my friend Hyman could come back to life and read the amount of times his term is used in the Congressional Record, why, Hyman would drop dead all over again. Talk about assimilation?"

"So you're saying that through cultural assimilation lots of what comes from black culture gets distributed to other countries through America's cultural colonization program," I asked.

"I didn't say it was a program. For the most part it just seems to happen.

It's probably because America is so far advanced technologically. But now that you've brought it up, maybe somewhere in a dingy little office in Washington, there is a suit sitting at a desk with that assignment."

"I shouldn't put these things in your head," I said.

"Another point I want to make is that lots of black cultural traits that other generation of whites used to frown on has gained acceptance and are now a part of mainstream culture."

"What kinds of things are you talking about," I asked.

"Things like break dancing, high five, rap music hair styles, inner city styles, black language, and so on. Today you would never have thought that these things were once solely black, borrowed occasionally by a small band of white people the writer Norman Mailer, once called 'the White Negroes".

"Listening to you, there must be more 'White Negroes' now than when Mailer coined the term. And, according to you, they will soon be all over the world sporting the latest in black-inner-city cultural styles."

"Not the very latest," Sleepy Willie said, "you see it takes a little time for the transformation to happen. For instance, it once took as long as thirty years for a black expression to reach the mainstream, now it happens in five years. If a hip black expression was coined in Harlem this morning, in five years you'll hear it in the halls of Congress. This is the sign that a black term has made it, when you hear politicians use it in public. Now you take the way these kids here in the South Bronx dress, you know, with their baggy pants hanging off their butts showing their drawers. Bronx kids wear these big hooded sweaters and sneakers. That

look is a fashion statement the world over. Big time fashion de-
signers come here to see how these kids in the South Bronx are
hooked-upped, then they run back to their drawing boards to get
in front of the curve."

"Willie, you mean to say that the black style is also driving
the fashion dollar?"

"But here is the joke," Willie said, "the whole concept comes
from the homeless people. You've seen guys sleeping on the subway in baggy pants they got from the homeless shelters. They
wear these oversize sweaters and coats to cover as much of themselves while they sleep. And when the cops chase them, their
pants fall and they drawers show while they try to gather their
belongings. These people are society's outcast. But still, somehow, our youth accepted this down and out look as stylishly cool."

"Why?" I asked.

"I think they were choosing sides," Willie said. Or maybe
they were preparing for their futures. Who knows? The style
caught on and now young people the world over dress alike.
Like I said, if it's hip in black America, it's hip in America. If it's
hip in America, it's what the rest of the world aspire."

" So youth of the world dress like homeless New York City
subway vagrants."

"In this case, that's what's hip in America," Willie said. "And
many of them never saw the insides of a subway car. Colonialism
is never a clean-cut business. Ain't that some funny shit?"

CONGRESSMEN AND SUITCASES

"That's it. My mind is made. There's no turning around. I'm gonna run for Congress," Sleepy Willie said.

I looked at Willie astonish by his audacity. "Willie what are you talking about. You don't have any experience in politics. I know you talk politics, but you've never shown any interest in being a legislator. Besides you're too old to get into politics."

"I don't want to legislate," Willie said, "I just want to be a congressman."

"Well," I said, reaching out into the darkness, "what brings on your sudden interest in the Congress?"

"Money," Willie said.

"Money?"

"Yeah, money, you know dead presidents."

"Go on," I said.

"Don't you know that there are business people and special interest groups who enlist congressmen to turn favors for them. When a businessman needs a favor he buys a suitcase and fills it up with money. Then he takes it to a fancy Washington hotel and call up the United States Congress. He tells them about the favor and the suitcase. The first congressman that arrives is the proud new owner of a suitcase . . . filled with dead presidents. I don't care how you try to discourage me; I want one of those suitcases. No, I want a complete set."

"I'm not going to try to discourage you, but do tell me how

would you get elected? Your name is not one that is widely known. You're not connected to any political club. Your only participation in politics in that you vote."

"You're right," Willie said, undaunted by my skepticism, "I'll just do what other candidates do to get campaign funds. I'll let the word get out to prospective contributors that when I get to Washington, they can pull the strings but I will open the suitcases."

"Oh, come on Willie, be realistic. Just where do you think you will find people like that?"

"In any number of the Fortune Five Hundred companies and a whole lot of smaller ones," Willie said.

"Man, I'm really disappointed that this kind of thinking is coming from you. Willie I don't mean any harm, but you're an old black man with absolutely no political experience. From what you say, your only qualification would be that you are on the take. Now who do you think will throw money in a situation like that?"

"Politics being politics," Willie said, "that's all I'll need. Now I'm not naïve enough not to know that I will have to dress in sheep clothing. I've got that covered too. I'll have to express some high sounding reasons for wanting to go to Washington. Mine will be to eliminate the waste and to make the government approachable."

"You want to eliminate what waste?"

"Let me tell you," Willie said, the idea sparking in his eye. "I will not go to Washington with the same wasteful habits the bums there now have. No way Jose. Not in this time, not in this day. I would start off by cutting some waste. When I got a call from, say, the National Riffle Association, saying they needed my vote on a bill to put hand guns in the hands of every American. I would mail them a suitcase out of courtesy and my desire to keep the cost of corruption down."

"But Willie, you hate the N.R.A. and Charston Heston."

"Yes, but I would feel the need to serve all the people. So I would send favor seekers a suitcase. But here is the gem in my scheme; I would recycle my suitcases. I would buy a closet full of suitcases at wholesale prices. I mail it out empty, it comes back full and, it's reusable. You know, graft is costly enough, taxpayers shouldn't have to pay extra for it. I could look every man; woman and child, in my district in the eye and say I want to cut the waste. Yes, that's a platform that could get me to Washington."

"I should hope not," I said, "not every congressman is dishonest you know."

"Find me an honest congressman," Willie bellowed, "and I'll show you the fellow I want to run against. An honest congressman would be a weak and unconnected congressman, a congressman without suitcases. A connected congressman would be strong and . . . willing to bend a little, a man who can open a suitcase. Now don't get me wrong. I ain't destining, I'm explaining, because you see, I want to be a congressman too."

"Willie, congressmen and women are elected to represent the people. They are the people's voice in government. They make the laws and bring hope and programs to the people. I think you're being entirely too sinister. You make it sound like every congressman in Washington is on the take."

"My point is this, " Willie said, "I want to be one of them. Now it's time to get my campaign started. I'm going to need some hard working people in my corner to share in the glory. I want a large staff, people who know about the stuff of favors and suitcases. Do you want to be my campaign manager?"

"Of course not. I wouldn't associate with the kind of public official you would be, thinking as you are."

"I'm crushed," Willie said, "I offer you a position of wealth, prestige and power and you return it with an insult."

"I don't mean to insult you Willie. I'm concern for you, don't you know you could go to jail. I can see the headline now: Congressman Sleepy Willie Walker Investigated for Bribery. Man, your political career is headed for ruin even before it gets off the ground. And you would end up in the slammer."

"Congressmen don't go to jail," Willie said, "they get censured and re-elected."

"Not all the time Willie. Some of them don't get re-elected. Some of them get tainted by the scandal they create and end up shunned. So you better think hard about what you would do if you got caught up in something like that, and didn't get re-elected. You would be right back where you started."

"I wouldn't be right back where I started. I would be ahead of the game because I would still have all those suitcases. The next headline you read would say: EX-Congressman Sleepy Willie Walker Goes into the Luggage Business."

WISHING OPRAH HAPPINESS

"**Y**ou know," Sleepy Willie said out of thin air, "America's most visible woman is also its most mysterious. Strange isn't it?"

"Let me guess who you're talking about," I said.

"You don't have to guess. I'll tell you, if you would just let me talk."

"Hillary Clinton?"

"Now Hillary Clinton is highly visible and there are some mysterious aspects to her public persona, but no."

"Then it's got to be Judge Judy?"

"No, I'm talking about Oprah Winfrey."

"Oprah Winfrey?"

"Bingo," Willie said.

"What's so mysterious about her? Oprah Winfrey is probably the best known person on television today. She is in the homes of twenty-two million viewers a week. She is seen talking with the most powerful people of our time and with common folks as well. All aspects of her life have been reviewed in tabloids and on talk shows including her own. We know about her being raped. We know about her love affair with Stedman."

"Stedman," Willie exclaimed, "is that his first name, or his last name. Stadman, maybe that's his only name, Stadman."

"We know who her best friends are," I continued. "We know what books she reads. We even know that she buys in bulk. We know that Maya Angelou is like her guru and the edification she receives make her comes through that television screen as THE ENLIGHTENED ONE. If there is one person in America who is truly known, that would be Oprah Winfrey. I'm a fan."

"So am I," Willie said, "she's done tons of good for all kinds of people. You know I'm a movie buff. The thing I most appreciate her for is that she continues to make movies without a mass appeal. I enjoy her movies and I often learn from her movies. But they don't make money and wouldn't be made if not for her. You know it was her film version of Toni Morrison's book 'Beloved' that gave me an understanding of the story on a second reading. Oprah's made life better for me and many of the world's people, but she's not done right by her own self."

"Willie, the woman is one of the wealthiest persons in America. She has an esteemed career. She can have anything and go anywhere she wants. She is the prefect role model for not only women, but also for entrepreneurs, and for people who seek enlightenment. She's built an empire. What do you mean that she hasn't done right by herself?"

"She's built a dynasty without a line of hereditary succession. When she's gone that's it. The government will swoop down on her fortune like hungry buzzards and eat up a fifty-five percent chunk. Everyone else who built fortunes large as hers bequest it to descendants who then stayed rich for generations. Oprah's legacy ends with her. There won't be any great grand children looking at a grand painting of the maternal founder of the dynasty in a grand gown studded with jewels hanging in the grand room of the family mansion and that's sad."

"After all that, you need to take a grand breath," I said. "That kind of self glorification is for other folks. I find it refreshing that Oprah doesn't need to flatter herself that way."

" Now you take the Mellons, the Vanderbilt's, the Rockefellers, the Gettys, the Hearst, these families built their fortunes back at the turn of the nineteenth century, but their legacy lives on generation after generation. I find it mysterious that Oprah isn't going all the way to build an empire that will last a century or two through her descendants. That's what empire building is all about, establishing a strong and powerful family to carry on a tradition."

"Willie, I don't see how that means she's not doing right by herself. I think that Oprah Winfrey's self-awareness is so keen, that everything she does is exactly what she wants to do. This woman practices self-awareness and methods of enlightenment. She is only where she wants to be. What are you talking about?"

"Children. Oprah Winfrey is passing through her childbearing age without having any children. That's a mystery to me"

"Willie, she never got married. There still are a few people old fashion enough to believe that children belong in marriages."

"Stop being silly," Willie said. "You've got to be curious why she hasn't gotten married or had children?"

"Willie I know lots of people who's never married. I know lots of people who have never had children. I know people who are married and don't have children. I even know people who have children and aren't married. But I don't find any of it mysterious. That's life."

"None of those folks you know have a net worth upwards of half a billion dollars. They're regular people—which take the mystery out of them. We are here talking about one of the richest women in the world. We're talking about a woman who can leave a family legacy, and the mystery, for me, is why she haven't taken that path."

"Oprah is a business woman. She's got to be one of the busiest persons on earth. She may have decided that she doesn't want a husband and family and the distractions what would bring to her busy and industrious life. There just ain't any mystery in that."

"Let me leave that alone." Willie said. "I can see that we're not going to come to terms on that score. Here is something else I find mysterious.'

"Good, another subject. Shoot."

"The same subject. It's a mystery to me how a childless black single woman can have the number one talk show on television, counseling, mostly white, married mothers on married life, raising children, and family life? Figure that."

"What's to figure Willie? What makes her show so popular has got be the high quality of the advice she dispenses."

"I asked you to stop being silly. Ecaroh, stick with me here. How is a person without any experience with a husband or children to give reasonable counsel to those living through that experience? You've got to see the irony there."

"Maybe there is some irony, but I don't find this mysterious, It's done all the time. Willie, We've got unmarried clergymen who counsel people on matters of family life and children. We've got unmarried, married counselors who administer to the problems of married couples."

"And in a Texas hospital they found a guy performing surgery on patients and the guy had never been to medical school."

I'm afraid Oprah's millions cloud your judgement about her. You want your favorite rich person to be what you want her to be, not what she is."

"People who can't swim don't give swimming lessons," Willie said. "You've got some money in the stock market, tell me, would you invest your money on the advice of someone who has no experience in the market?"

"Oprah's got a gift and she is sharing it with the world. Her unique position in life has given her a special insight on the ways of the world and that is what she gives to her viewers. I believe that it's possible to be rich and still be caring and generous."

"Which bring us back to the central point and that is what does Oprah do for Oprah? We see her on television and she looks so happy and knowledgeable, but that's subterfuge. That's barren bullshit. We're not getting what we see in this case. I believe Oprah would be happier if she was a mother in the projects with three or four kids, an ex-husband and an abusive boyfriend. Her life would be hard, but real. You talk about her being a person of

Sleepy Willie Sings the Blues

enlightenment, the great Zen Masters say that enlightenment empties you so that you can be filled with the stuff of life. A husband and some crumb-snatchers to carry her legacy would fill Oprah's life."

"Oh, come on Willie, you can't mean that. You just said that the chance for happiness is higher for a single mother in the projects than it is for a rich and glamorous television personality. I've heard enough; you're off your rocker. If you could, you would trade places with Oprah Winfrey. Tell me, would you trade places with a single mother in the projects? I've heard how you talk about some single moms in the projects."

"I mean the ones struggling back to make it," Willie said

"Even so, if you had to would you rather trade places with one of them or Oprah Winfrey?"

"Oprah's life just seem so sterile, too sterile for any happiness to be there. I'd just like to see her with the legacy of descendant to carry on her tradition and to authenticate her family counseling. Believe me Ecaroh, I'm only wishing Oprah happiness."

"Sounds like sour grapes to me."

"I'm only wishing Oprah happiness."

FAGGOT

"Well there you have it," I said to Sleepy Willie. "Now they have a policy to keep gays in the military. Don't ask, don't tell. The world is changing faster and farther than I would have imagine."

"I ain't never served in the military," Willie said. "But I know a faggot or two who has served. The American military, far as I know, haven't suffered any from their service."

"Willie, I don't understand you. Why you're not even sensitive enough to refer to them as gays—or at least—homosexuals and you're in favor of them serving in the military."

"That's because I'm not a hypocrite. There are some facts of life that will run you over if you don't get out of its way. Faggots are everywhere. They are as much a part of life as air pollution, you don't like it, but you know that that won't make it go away. You know, there was a faggot who used to come in this very bar. He behaved like every body else, he bought his drink and drank it. He never tried to pick-up sex partners in the bar— far as I know—but I can't say the same for the straight people who come here. There were some people who snickered behind his back, but for the most part, he was accepted as a fellow bar stool sitter,"

"Wow! Willie, he sounds just right for the marines," I said having some fun.

"Well, he must have been," Willie said, "because he joined

the marines in 1968. He spent two weeks home before he went off to the war in Vietnam. Came right into this bar, wearing his sharply pressed uniform. He had some friends with him, they had some drinks and lots of laughs. And in a short time he was off to the war. People in the bar thought he'd became a medic or paper pusher. They made jokes about him being in faggot's paradise among all those tough marines and they make up newspaper headlines describing the scandalous activities he would engage in. You know how these people think and talk."

"I never thought about it, but I guess there were gays who fought in Vietnam."

"Fought and died," Willie corrected, "and not just in Vietnam, but every military conflict this country has had. It's not a well-known fact and it's something people don't talk about because of the taboo, but it's nothing new. Modern faggots want to serve and die if necessary, without being questioned."

"Willie, I just don't think the country's ready for this. The average Joe on the street doesn't want any part of a military with gays in it. Then there is the whole question of how far society will go in accepting gays into the mainstream. You've heard of the Christian Coalition and you know the exclusive lean of the conservative far right, man there ain't no way gays in the military is gonna fly."

"Hypocrites! They're all hypocrites," Willie said. If there was a war important enough to these hypocrites, they would be drafting everybody they could—including your mama."

"Willie, why do you have to use my mother as often as you do to make your points?'

"It ain't nothing personal, " Willie said. "I met your mama at your house on a Christmas day a few years back. You remember? Man we all had a good time—and your mama—if I was a few years younger, man . . ."

"Willie . . ."

"Forget it man. I'm just playing with you. Seriously, these people railing against homosexuals want to think that their position put them on the moral high ground. It's there that they can hide their fear and their ignorance, their hatred, and their bigotry.

It's homophobia hiding behind morality. If these so-called Christians want to hold the moral high ground, they would be feeding the hungry, clothing the needed, and spreading the word of the Gospel."

"Spreading the word is what they would say they are doing by opposing homosexuality. They use the bible to make their point—they quote the words of the Holy Scriptures, Willie they claim God as an ally."

Willie raised his near empty beer glass in the air to single the barmaid for another round.

"God don't abandon none of his children," Willie said, "I always worry for people who claim that God is on their side. I worry for them, but I fear for their opponents. Folks who claim God as a team Captain are capable of doing anything."

"Okay Willie. What happened to the fellow you were telling me about?"

"He's dead."

"Dead? Well what happened—how did he die?"

"He died a war hero. He was the point man for his company in a search and destroy mission. The Vietcong had laid an ambush for the company of marines. They would always let the point man through to get to the main body of the patrol; they'd get him later. From what I heard, our South Bronx hero sensed something was wrong. And although he didn't see anyone, he opened fire to warn his company that they were walking into an ambush. He was shot dead immediately, he must have known he would be, but he wanted to save the lives of the hundred or more men in his company. Those who know about this, say that his company was able to deploy and get themselves out of a bad situation. Now I'd bet none of those men in that combat situation would say that they oppose homosexuals in the military—at least not that homosexual."

"That's some story," I said, "but people would say, well that's just one."

"They would have to tell me," Willie said, " how many of the fifty thousand names on the Vietnam War Memorial are names of gay soldiers? Is it anything like the percentage of gays in the general population? Then what will they do? They can't erase the names of faggots who died in the service of their country, no more than they can erase their brave deeds. I'm not going to ask the hypocrites 'cause I don't want them to tell me."

496-MUNG

ORANGE PEOPLE

"**I** was talking to this orange woman at the seniors center the other day," Sleepy Willie said, "and I have concluded that orange people just don't get it. They misunderstand themselves, they misunderstand black folks, and they misunderstand our mutual predicament."

"Willie before you tell me what it is orange people don't get, please tell me what kind of people are orange people and even more importantly, what were you doing at the senior center?"

"I'm a senior citizen, so I should be able to stop by the center once in a while without being questioned about it."

"I asked because I just didn't think this senior citizen thing was your style," I said.

"Enough on that," Willie said. "Orange people are the people the rest of the world refer to as white."

"I thought that's where you would go with that. You have taken it upon yourself to rename white people—orange—is that it Willie?"

"I like to call a spade a spade. I ain't ever seen but one white person in all my life. All of the people who call themselves white are really kind of orangy. White people are more orange than white. If you don't believe me here is a simple test you can do that will convince you. Take a sheet of white paper and an orange and put it up next to the skin of every so-called white person you come in contact with and see which color match closest. Now I'm not being derogatory or any of that, I'm just calling a spade a spade."

"That would be a simple test indeed," I said. "I could never put any of my white friends through that kind of humiliation."

"White people are orange and I'm telling you it's so. The only white person I ever saw was a white man who worked in a cemetery. Late one night I was riding the 'A' train back from Lefferts Boulevards. This fellow who must have been digging a grave got on the train at the station stop by the cemetery before the train goes back under the ground. You know that big cemetery that the 'A' train goes by?

"Yeah," I said, "the one at the Boyd Avenue station stop."

"Okay," Willie continued, "Well this man got on the train at that station right above the cemetery. He wore a sloppy cap, a denim jacket, gray work pants, and muddy boots, but the thing that I notice most was his whiteness. Man, this cat was white as a sheet; I mean white like snow. The whitest man in the world, you hear me? Looking at him sent shivers down my spine. I looked around and for the first time realized that I was the only other person in that car. I felt the fear that seeing a truly white man can bring. I couldn't tell whether he worked at the cemetery or lived there. That was a white, white man. Most other so-called white people are orange and they ought to be glad—a snow white man is an ugly thing, so ugly and creepy, in fact, so-called white people ought to discourage the use of the designation. I've seen truly black, black people and they are beautiful, but a truly white person, and I mean white like snow, is a terribly sight."

"Willie," I asked, somewhat desperately, "what happen with the lady at the senior's center?"

"You asked me a question about orange people," Willie said. "You ask, I explain."

"I should have known better," I said.

"This orange woman was talking about black people's attitude. She feels black people bring a lot of white backlash on themselves and she told me so. She said that just because many bad things had been done to black people, this was no reason for black people to walk around with chips on their shoulders. Get over it, she told me. Stand up and take control of your own lives. I couldn't contain myself; I had to tell that old woman my truth. 'Ms. Weldon' I said, 'you are very, very, lucky that all we do have on our shoulders are chips. My dear Ms. Weldon, if what has befallen our race had, instead, befallen your race, why your people would not have chips on their shoulder, your people would have machine guns on their shoulders. So you are fortunate indeed that the shoulders of Sun People carry only chips and not machine guns.' "

"That's to the bone stuff Willie. How did this lady take being told your truth?"

"Of course, she denied orange people would seek justice with guns. She don't remember a thing about their past history, she went off talking about all the violence among black youths. I told her just like I saw it. The outlaw attitude among some of my people results from the feeling of alienation. What's happening in the black community is a bad and misdirected imitation of Caucasian behavior. The black community is reacting in a knee-jerk manner to planned poverty and pauperism.

"Oh my, why did I have to say that. Ms. Weldon lit into me about her not wanting to hear the myth about how poverty breeds crime. Now I have always recognized this to mean that black people are innately criminal. I had no intentions to hurt the feeling of an old misinformed orange woman, but I had to remain true to myself. I asked her to take a look at Russia, I believed she is a second generation American of Russian descent and I wanted her to be able to relate to my rap in a most personal way. Read *The New York Times*, I told her, look at how all those orange people over there are killing up each other. When Russia was a part of the Soviet Union, there was crime to be sure, but now that the oppression of communism has past and the people can see the true disparities in the distribution of wealth, Russia has become a country of criminals. The Times carries stories about Russian boys shooting other Russian boys dead for a pair of American sneakers. Russian gangsters are killing each other in the streets. Drug use is on the raise, and prostitution is wide

ONE WORLD ECONOMY

"You can't find a thing in the stores that was made in America these days," Sleepy Willie said. "Last week I went downtown to 34th. Street to do a little shopping. Man, all the stores are filled to the brim with goods from Peru, Mexico, Thailand, Korea, China, Brazil, Hong Cong, and the Philippine. Any place but the USA. It is nearly impossible to fine something made in America. Now you know I'm an old union man and I empathize with the American worker, unionized or not, when it comes to American jobs going overseas. The government and the captains of American industry are selling Americans workers out and I don't like it.

"The world's money barons have discovered yet another way to maximize profits and they're going global with it. Yes, they're playing big-time now. They're manipulating the world's labor force by pitting worker against worker. The American money barons are moving their manufacturing operations to poor world countries where they can pay workers a dollar a day for doing jobs that American workers made livable wages doing. All these money barons hear is the sound of their cash registers, clink, clink. The whole purpose of every worker is to make the people at the top richer and richer. The world's production systems are being structured to turn the largest profits at the lowest cost. In America, workers have to be provided pension packages, health care insurance, sick days, unemployment benefits, paid holidays, including Martin Luther King's birthday. American Money barons don't want to hear that song any more, so they take their operations and their jobs to Peru. Clink, Clink. So you think that goods produced in Peru by dollar a day laborers would cost less? You think the money barons would share the windfall with American consumers? Think again. Clink, clink. The world's workers will have to suffer a generation of money barons with ultimate greed.

"What we see here is the triumph of capitalism and it ain't pretty, least not for American workers. Slim Johnson use to make $13.50 an hour working for a company that makes computer keyboards. The company moved to Mexico. Now Pancho Villa does the same job for $1.20 a day. The keyboard that Slim Johnson worked on cost $61.27 to produce and had a retail value of $259.00. Pancho's keyboard cost $14.83 to produce, with a retail value of $259.00. Slim Johnson's got a daughter in college who needs a computer, but he can't buy her one because he is out of work. His job went to Pancho Villa in Mexico, whose daughter also could use a computer. Pancho's got a job, but he can't afford to buy her one—he doesn't make enough. That ought to bring a—I told you so—to the face of Karl Marx.

"You see, the huge reduction in the cost of labor, plus the complete reduction of the cost of benefits for the workers, doesn't go to reduce the retail cost of the keyboard, it goes into the pockets of stock holders. Wall-Streeters are calling the tune the worlds workers have to dance too. Now I'm sure that the people in these poor countries are glad for the jobs, at first, because they don't realize that they are being ripped-off. Most of them were poor and not working, now they're working, but still poor. They see capitalism at work in their lives and hope for a brighter future. But the triumph of capitalism means another whole thing for the American worker. The American worker is on a downward turn and will one day receive the wage that Pancho works for—taco change."

"Now just wait a minute Willie," I said, "I've let you run on long enough, throwing around phrases like One World Economy, Triumph of Capitalism, and you even mentioned Karl Marx. Surely you know that the collapse of the Soviet Union proves the communist economic system was inferior to the great economic engine of capitalism. Americans have the highest standard of living of any people on earth. And I don't know what you know about Karl Marx, but his system of socialism has not worked—in Russia, nor China, or in Cuba. Willie the socialist system of production and distribution has been forever defeated."

"Yeah," Willie said, "And now the tension is gone."

"What tension?" I asked.

"The tension between capitalism and socialism. The pull and tug that both sides jerked the rest of the world around with. That tension kept the world separated economically and that created competition that gave the most productive workers high wages. While they were two dueling systems the money barons in the capitalist system had to control their greed to show that capitalism was the system that would raise the living standards of workers. Now that one side has collapsed, the one that's standing is calling the tune and the money barons has unlashed their greed. One system has got a monopoly on the world's workers. In this one world economy there is no tension, no competition between systems and the workers suffers from it."

"Willie, what I hear you saying is that the return of communism would be a good thing."

"The tension between the two systems worked something like necessary parts of a whole, like yin and yang. And you know you can't have yin without yang, you can't have in without out, you can't have hot without cold, in all of life there has to be that counter balance. Now there is no counter balance to capitalism and the world's workers are getting the shaft."

"Well Willie, if nobody's making any money who's going to buy the things industrialist make? A system of yin without yang is doomed."

"You're exactly right," Willie said, "but there is going to be some suffering before the American worker revolt and start a world wide movement to fight for workers rights—and there is going to be some blood in the streets, all the streets of the world. Workers are going to rise to demand fair labor treatment and equity in the work place."

"Willie, man, I really don't mean to demean any thing you've said, because there is something wrong going on. I've just got to tell you that that line you just ran down sounds like it came from out of the movie "Reds." Or maybe from some speech during the Russian revolution, we've heard all of that before."

"That's because what comes around goes around. Workers of the world unite; you've also heard that before " Willie said.

BILL CLINTON'S AMERICA

"He tried to take us there," Sleepy Willie said, "but the distance was too great and the time too short."

Who tried to take us where?" I asked.

"Bill Clinton," Willie said. "He had a vision of what he wanted America to become. We gave him eight years to take us there— to Bill Clinton's America. Ah, but the distance was too far to travel in a mere eight years. There are just too many Americans who want to keep too many other Americans down, plus, there were some major bumps on the way—but, all in all, Bill took us a considerable part of the way. At the very least, he moved us a safe distance from Ronald Reagan's America."

"Bill Clinton's America, Willie what is Bill Clinton's America? Or should I ask, where is Bill Clinton's America?"

"Like I said, we didn't reach it, but if we had, this would be an America where health care is available to all of those who go without it this evening. Clinton tried—put his old lady in charge of that one and the train never left the station. But, you know, even with all the money and malice thrown against her, Hillary's efforts wasn't a complete failure. Today, even the opponents of health care—can you imagine what kind of mama jamma would oppose health care—even they now admit that there has to be some movement towards Bill Clinton's America on health care. During the days of the civil rights movement, Martin Luther King knew that if he could expose the brutality of Bull Conners, people would be repulsed and they would cry out for change. The HMO's are acting like Bull Conners and now people want change and protection from them.

"If we had reached Bill Clinton's America on gun control, it would be an America without school shootings, or, children shooting children, or, easy access to hand guns, or, guns without safety locks. This would be an America where only law-abiding citizens would be able to purchase a handgun and even they would have to register their guns every year. Clinton signed the Brandy Bill into law, but Bill Clinton's America, on gun control was not reached. And do you know why? Because the National Rifle Association and all the money they used to buy, that's right, buy, the votes of congressmen and congresswomen on gun control issues. Plus, we got millions of gun nuts who say they have to arm themselves against the possible tyranny of the government, the United States government, you hear me? The N.R.A.'s got a membership of three million well-armed paranoid kooks equipping themselves to do battle with their United States government. These white boys say they stay armed to the teeth to prevent the advent of a totalitarian government. Now if white people fear their government and feel they must arm themselves against it, what do you think we ought to be doing? I mean if there is any group in America who needs to fear the government, besides communist, which group would you think that is? Surely not some burly white boys in Montana who want to print their own money.

"Now we reached Bill Clinton's America on the economy . . . well, nearly. Never before in the history of man, has there been such heights of prosperity. No matter what, though, the rich always get richer. There has been the largest increase in new millionaires ever. People are getting rich who haven't been rich before. Now that don't say much for those of us who didn't make our fortune during the Clinton economic boom, just like the rich always get richer, the poor always get poorer. But we benefited from low inflation and all the new jobs created during the Clinton years. Things would have been even better for the working poor

129

if Ron Brown had lived and Robert Reich stayed on with Clinton. This was not to be. Still, Clinton can say he put a chicken in every pot and a computer in every home . . . well, almost.

"We didn't reach bill Clinton's America on race either. Now you know that racial relation is the biggest issue in America today. It always was and continues to be. No one can say that Clinton didn't try. He tried to move America forward on race relation in the best way, by example. He formed a government that had more minority people in positions of responsibility than any president before him. He was showing the corporate world what they should look like. That it's possible to be fair in hiring practice and competent in business policies at the same time. Bill Clinton tapped the black community for it's smartest, strongest, most articulate, and, I might add, best dressed. Bill Clinton headed an administration that, at the very least, acknowledged the existence of the black community. Now that was a very important thing for the reconciliation of ordinary black and white people—and while some pretty horrific racial acts happened during the Clinton years, the dialogue goes on. And for many ordinary people, race is becoming less of a factor. Oh, sure, we still have a long way to go in this country, but give it a little time, and a few more presidents like Bill Clinton and we might get there. Yeah, we're going to need more governors, mayors, legislators, and corporate leaders who won't resist the idea of a fair and equable America in order to reach Bill Clinton's America on race."

"All that you've said is true," I said, "but I hope you haven't forgotten the fact that there isn't a single black governor or United States senator."

"That's coming," Willie said. "We've got some rising stars in the Congress and in state legislatures all over the country. These are the people who will further the job Bill Clinton didn't finish. They may not take us to Bill Clinton's America, because they have their own vision of what America ought to be, but it won't be far off."

WILLIE GOES TO CHURCH

"**D**o you remember I told you a while back that I'm seeing this lady from my old neighborhood every so often. She now
lives a few blocks from me, here in The South Bronx," Sleepy
Willie said.

"Yeah, of course, I remember. I've just never asked about
her to give you your privacy on that matter. You told me her
name is Mrs. Regina Brentwood and that you've had many a
Sunday dinners with her. And, this is the lady that you've spent
the New Year with for the past several years."

"Well, I'm glad that's all I told you. You remember too well
and too much. Anyway that woman makes a powerful pot of collard greens, you hear me boy. No pork in them greens. Mrs.
Brentwood, that is how I address her and she calls me Mr. Walker,
seasons her greens with smoke turkey wings. Good greens, you
hear me."

"Yeah, I hear you, but I think there is something else you
want to tell me about this affair."

"Well yes," Willie said, "her fried chicken would put the
Colonel out of business. There would still be automats restau-
rants if they made macaroni and cheese like she does. You hear
me."

"Yeah," I said, "'Mrs. Brentwood can cook. Willie you are a
lucky man to be keeping company with a woman that can please
your palate, and whatever else."

"I ain't saying that there is any 'whatever else.' Her cooking does please me, but now she has taken sight to saving my soul. She had been trying to get me to go to church with her for about a year now. I've been able to get out of it by promising that I would. That worked well until a few weeks ago. Sunday before last, I called to let her know I was on my way for dinner."

"You had to call before you went?" I asked.

"I don't care how old a single woman is, if you're a real man you'll call before you go."

"Point taken," I said.

"Man I was hungry and ready to grease. When I got there the stove was cold and there wasn't a pot in sight, no plates on the table . . . nothing, you hear me. When I asked her what the score was, she said, 'Mr. Walker, Reverend Brown preached a sermon last week that inspired me to lay the facts on you today.' Well to make a long story short, I recognized my shortcomings on the spot. I took her out to dinner that night and made a solemn promise to go to church the very next Sunday, which was last week. At ten o'clock Sunday morning I arrived at Mrs. Brentwood's apartment and we took a cab down to Mount Olive Baptist Church on one hundred and twenty-second street and Malcolm X Boulevard in Harlem."

"No Willie," I protested, "back up. Don't make a long story short. I want to know what Mrs. Brentwood said that made you go to church."

"It wasn't anything she said, it was the thought of not having her collard greens and fried chicken."

"So you went to church to protect your stomach."

"Mrs. Brentwood has been a member of Mount Olive for almost fifty years. She is on almost all of its committees and she knows everyone in the church," Willie said ignoring my comment about his stomach. "We arrived well before service began and she took me to this group and that saying this is Mr. William Walker introducing me to people. I have never felt so out of place and didn't want to be there, but I like collard greens seasoned with smoked turkey wings, and I like the company of Mrs. Brentwood, so I smiled and nodded to everyone she took me too."

"And?"

"Well because she is such an important member of the church we sat in the second pew right behind the Deacons and Senior Sisters of the church. Man I'm glad I had on my best suit, them cats were sharp and their women were clean too, you hear me. I haven't been to church for so long that I had forgotten about the sweet sound of gospel music. Mount Olive is a huge church with a balcony level and a high dome ceiling. The choirs sit in the rear of the balcony level. That dome ceiling distributes the sound of those choirs as if from on High. Mount Olive has six different choirs Mrs. Brentwood told me. They sing gospel in every style from the high brow operatic to the earthy sound of the Dixie Humming Birds. Two of the six choirs sang the Sunday I was there. Man those choirs rocked that building. One moment they had the sisters jumping in the aisle, the next moment, the sisters were shouting the joys of the Holy Spirit. Man they even sang a song that brought a tear to my eye."

"Well it sounds like you got more than collard greens and fried chicken out of this experience," I said.

"This was indeed an experience," Willie said. "I was of the mind that all preachers preached about come from the scriptures of the Bible. Well that is how it had been it all the other churches I had ever attended. At least this is how I had remembered it. This preacher preached about things that are going on in the city and in the country. He used stories in the Bible to make a contrast with what's going down now. This was no pie in the sky—you'll get your glory later in heaven preacher, no sir, this preacher was talking about glory and happiness right here, right now."

"Willie, you sound pretty worked up. All this from your love for collard greens. Life's twist and turns never cease to surprise me." I said.

"Well when church let out we mingled for a while," Willie continued, "and I got to tell you, I felt a lot more comfortable. And I felt it inside and outside of myself. I felt like I was in the right place, among the right people. One of Mrs. Brentwood's church brothers and his wife, who also live in The Bronx, gave us a ride back to Mrs. Brentwood's apartment building in their nice automobile. I spent the afternoon reading the Sunday papers and watching a little television while Mrs. Brentwood preformed her magic in the kitchen. Besides the chicken and the collard greens, and the macaroni, she surprised me with a pound cake that made me go out for ice cream. I washed the dishes and after we watched 60 Minutes, I went home a happy and contented man."

"See that," I said, "and you spent all that energy trying not to do something that turned out to be pleasant. Let me buy you another beer."

"No thanks," Willie said." One's fine for me tonight got to go to church tomorrow."

JERRY! JERRY! JERRY!

When I arrived at the bar last Friday afternoon. Sleepy Willie was sitting at the curve end of the bar watching television. Willie was the only other person in the bar asides from the barmaid, who was busy preparing for the evening crowd. The Jerry Springer show was signing off with his fans confessing their love for him and letting Jerry know that he is the bomb. Three young girls declared that they had come all the way from Detroit to see Jerry, when I entered Willie's consciousness.

"Ecaroh, man what are you doing here so early?"

"I didn't work today. I had some business downtown to attend too. I just stopped by on the way home," I said, as I walked towards our usual table.

"Come here," Willie said. "Sit at the bar, Oprah is coming on next."

"So this is how you spend your day huh? Watching the Jerry Springer show. Man you should be at the library reading Ralph Ellison's Invisible Man, or at the museum studying the evolution of man, or doing anything that would make better use of your mind and time."

"Ecaroh, don't be one of those old fuddy-duddies who don't recognize the social redeeming qualities of the Jerry Springer show."

"You're joking, I know you are."

"About what?"

"The social redeeming qualities of the Jerry Spinger show."

"That's no joke. That's a sociological declaration."

"No doubt one from a pseudo-sociologist. Willie, the Jerry Springer show is the epitome of junk television. A show by the mindless, for the mindless."

"I'm not going to spent anytime defending what I watch on television, but if you want me to, I will explain what good Jerry Springer does."

"Impossible," I said, "but I've got a minute."

"Well, for starters," Willie began, "Springer gives television exposure to a class of people who, until Springer, couldn't do anything but watch other classes of people on television. All scripted television portraits every American social class but one. All real-life television portraits all but one American social class. The television industry gears its programming towards a white upper-middle-class audience. Springer is giving the underclass of America a piece of the action. A place where they can make their existence known. The Jerry Springer Show represents the democratization of the airwaves."

"William F. Buckley jr. would be so proud of what you just did with words."

"What's Buckley got to do with this?"

"You just best him in the ability to dress foul purpose in high sounding platitudes. You just said that Springer, by presenting a bunch of trailer-trash psychopaths on television, is democratizing who is seen on television."

"Even despicable ignoramuses have rights to the airwaves. You don't have to like them; you don't have to watch them. All you've got to do is remember that the airwaves belong to the people, all the people. Secondly, the Springer show is exposing the myth that African Americans are the only group with an underclass. Yes, Americans think that blacks have a monopoly on the lowlifes of this country. But I watch Springer and find that there is a deep white underclass in America. Jerry Springer found them and now he brings them into the consciousness of television viewers all over the world."

"Willie are you telling me that before the Springer show, you didn't know that there are ignorant uncouth white people in this country?"

"I've known it, but its been hidden. It's not been a part of the American consciousness like the black underclass. I see the black underclass in the movies, on television, on the news, in newspapers, and in my neighborhood twenty-four/seven. We see the black underclass so often that for many people they are the icons for all black people. But until Springer, the white underclass has been like America's dirty little secret. Images of the black underclass are firmly formed in our mass consciousness, but what we see of the white underclass is, to many, educational. Springer is giving television viewers a tutorial on the true demographic of American society. This second point makes the Springer show both democratizing and educational. On Springer, we see a piece of Americana that's been out of the spot light."

"Well . . . I, I" I started to say something, but I didn't have a point. "I don't know where they find these people who go on that show and act the way they do and express the things they express." This wasn't what I intended to say, at first, but it was something.

"Right here," Willie said, "in the dirty little crevices and abyss of American society. You don't think they come from another planet, do you? This too is America, to paraphrase somebody."

"Willie, I just don't understand how you find such trash worth watching, socially redeeming or not."

"I just told you two very valid reasons why Springer belongs to television. Do you contradict them?"

"They do what you say they do, but are they enough reasons to give this kind of television a pass?"

"In addition to those points, maybe you ought to look at the ratings. Man there is a lot of people watching that 'trash,' as you put it, every single show. Now this is how the television marketplace works. Give the people what they want to watch and go to the bank."

137

"Yeah, I admit that lots of folks watch Springer, but I'll never figure out how this kind of junk survives."

"Because it has an audience. Which brings me to a final point. The Springer show gives viewers the opportunity to feel superior to the people featured on the show and the people in the audience, and, for some people, even to Springer himself. I believe that many people watch the Springer show to feed their need to feel chosen and above the losers on the show. The most often asked question about the Jerry Springer show is where do they find these people? Like nobody knows anybody, anything like the people we see on the show. We all come from somewhere else. This is all an expression of mass pomposity. The Jerry Springer show gives some people other people to feel superior too."

"For me Willie, I don't think it's a matter of feeling better than the nuts on the show as much as it is just not wanting that kind of show on television. They need to try something else less trashy."

"All of these talk shows spring from one very good one, the Phil Donahue show, but only two of them has defined thier audience. The Oprah Winfrey show knows its audience, and the Jerry Springer show knows its audience. Oprah gives them books, enlightenment, and family fare. Jerry gives them the underbelly of life. Montel, Sally, Queen Latifah, Jenny, and all the rest of them flounder in the rear of the ratings war. You want to know something, I believe that many of the people who complain about Jerry Springer watch the show secretly by themselves. Have you ever watched the show?"

"No, not really."

"So how did you form your opinion on it?"

"Well, I've seen some of it, I watched some of it a few different times . . . but I never watched an entire show. You don't need to watch an entire show to be repulsed by it, just like you don't have to eat all of a bad tasting meal to tell you don't like it."

open. Corruption is the bread of the nation. All of this, my dear lady, is happening in a nation of orange people. This, my dear Ms. Weldon is the results of poverty and disparity in a nation of orange people. Can there be a better place to study the effects of poverty and disparity and leave race out of it?"

"Willie," I said" I believe you said what you say you said, but I hope you didn't go into the orange people thing with that poor lady."

"No, not at length" Willie said, "because she thinks she's white, and I'm gonna let her sleep."

ONE WORLD ECONOMY

"You can't find a thing in the stores that was made in America these days," Sleepy Willie said. "Last week I went downtown to 34th. Street to do a little shopping. Man, all the stores are filled to the brim with goods from Peru, Mexico, Thailand, Korea, China, Brazil, Hong Cong, and the Philippine. Any place but the USA. It is nearly impossible to fine something made in America. Now you know I'm an old union man and I empathize with the American worker, unionized or not, when it comes to American jobs going overseas. The government and the captains of American industry are selling Americans workers out and I don't like it.

"The world's money barons have discovered yet another way to maximize profits and they're going global with it. Yes, they're playing big-time now. They're manipulating the world's labor force by pitting worker against worker. The American money barons are moving their manufacturing operations to poor world countries where they can pay workers a dollar a day for doing jobs that American workers made livable wages doing. All these money barons hear is the sound of their cash registers, clink, clink. The whole purpose of every worker is to make the people at the top richer and richer. The world's production systems are being structured to turn the largest profits at the lowest cost. In America, workers have to be provided pension packages, health care insurance, sick days, unemployment benefits, paid holidays,

CHANGING AMERICA

was off for the holiday. It was a nice sunny Labor Day. The marchers paraded down Fifth Avenue. The banks were closed and the subway trains ran on a holiday schedule. A third of the city's people were out of town celebrating the last holiday of the summer season. The air in recreation areas around the city carried the scents of grilled ribs, chicken, hamburgers, and hot dogs. Willie and I bought pastrami sandwiches and sodas from the Courthouse Deli to lunch in the park. The leaves of the trees in the park had autumn colors. The day had the feel of summer and the look of fall. We settled on a bench across the street from the courthouse. From this spot we would watch the world go by. This is where you'll see people from all over the Bronx. All races, sexes, socio-economic groups. This is where one meets a jury of one's peers when one goes afoul of the law. This is where the best pastrami sandwiches are assembled in this section of the Bronx. The Court House Deli, on the Southwest corner from the Bronx County Court House. People from all over The Bronx County are summons there five days a week to serve jury duty. Watch the people milling around the courthouse and you're offered a fairly good measure of The Bronx's demography. Willie and I sat on a park bench with a good view of the entire north side of the courthouse. But this day the courthouse was closed for business and the area was near deserted.

"I remember the days when mostly white folk came through

those doors." Willie said, looking towards the locked courthouse doors. "They didn't call Negroes for jury duty back then."

"All that's changed now," I said.

"More than that has changed. There are more different kinds of people in the Bronx now than could have been imagined thirty years ago. When I moved here from Manhattan thirty years ago, the Bronx was basically white, black, and Puerto Rican. The whites were composed of second generation, Italians, Irish, and Jews, mostly working class people striving towards that house in the suburbs. The blacks were mostly late comers; fresh from the South who couldn't find accommodations in an over crowded Harlem. The Puerto Ricans were pleased to squeeze in any place in the city. That's all they were, but even then, you could feel the winds of change hovering above the Bronx like a cleansing rain."

I took a bite from my sandwich and listened as Willie talked on.

"The Jews sold their soda and newspaper shops to the Arabs and moved up to Westchester County. The Italians sold their fish markets to the Koreans and moved to Yonkers. The Irish sold their vegetable stands also to the Koreans and moved to Long Island."

"That's for the most part true, but there are still Jews and Italians and Irish people living in the Bronx. Even a few Germans and Polish people are still here."

"Nothing is absolute," Willie said. "As the bulk of these people were leaving the Bronx, in came the Dominicans, the Colombians, the Haitians, the Jamaicans, and the new merchant class; the Arabs and the Koreans. And now the children of all these new arrivals to the Bronx go to school together, hang out together, visit each others homes, date, marry, and change the face of the Bronx."

"Diversity," I said. "You're talking about the shifting racial demographic of the Bronx, but more than that, you talking about the increase attitude of tolerance. Younger people today are far more tolerant of people from different backgrounds than in previous generations. People are diversifying."

"That's the word to explain what's going on in America today," Willie said. "The diversity that has taken place in the South Bronx is happening all over the country. America has finally given birth to a generation that seems to be tolerant enough of each other to begin a true melting pot process. And that's happening through the mixing of the races. It goes without saying, but I have never seen so many mixed race kids as there are today. The combinations are endless and the numbers are shocking."

"You're against race mixing?" I asked.

"When it was mostly a question of black and white, I felt blacks who made more than fifty grand a year should marry within the race to solidify the black middle-class. I was tired of seeing high wage earning blacks marrying whites to sort of underline the status of their financial position. It was like marrying white was a way of confirming financial success. So I was never against mixed marriages."

"Sounds to me like you're saying, you're not against poor blacks marrying white, but you are against blacks with money marrying white."

"Yeah, but I didn't come to that by racial means. I saw it purely as an economical fundamental. You know that it is the black middle-class that will bring prosperity to the race. The less polluted the black middle-class remains, the stronger it will be to help poorer blacks reach the middle-class. Many whites that are against race mixing are against it purely on the basis of race. That's racism. I'm no racist."

"You're an economic separatist who would engineer racial patterns through the pocketbook."

"I said these were my feeling when it was just a question of black and white," Willie said. "The wide spread racial mixing that's going on today will, in time, erase much of what is black, white, and everything else. And, it's going to change people's attitude on the whole question of race. It's one of those things that won't be stopped."

"So you think that racial mixing is going to eradicate racism?"

" I think it's changing people's attitudes," Willie said. "I read a story in a newspaper about a white Southern woman whose daughter was seeing a black fellow. The woman was furious. She fought with her daughter all the time about dating this black fellow. Things between them got so bad that the daughter moved out of the house and eventually wound up living with the black boyfriend. The woman felt ashamed and betrayed. She knew her neighbors were ridiculing her. Her pride kept her from having any contact with her daughter. Anyway, the couple wound up having a baby. The woman's worse fear had come true. She was tormented with the prospects of losing her daughter forever. The woman finally broke down and invited the daughter and the baby to visit, absent the father. Over a few such visits, the woman fell in love with the baby. She started keeping the baby while her daughter worked and now she thinks the world of this baby that came out a situation she was adamantly opposed too. Now she will cuss out any neighbor she hears saying disparaging things about her daughter or grandchild. This woman's attitude changed. America is changing."

"What about the boyfriend?"

"The article said that the woman was learning to be civil with him and will one day fully accept him as a part of her family."

"You'd settled for that?" I asked.

"Measure that against what existed twenty years ago and you'll find progress. Measure that against what will be twenty years from now and you'll see we've got a way to go. But let me tell you, all of this is relative, people of my generation remember back when there were few black celebrities. And no black movie stars. Don't get me wrong, there were lots of fine actors, male and female, who could have been stars. They had talent, but they didn't have the complexion that got them the connections. When people from my generation compare our times to what exist today, we see a huge improvement. Today we have black celebrities from just about any field you can imagine. Today there are black public figures who are admired and look up too by white people"

143

"Yeah," I agreed, "but when will we win the big prize?"

"You mean the presidency?" Willie asked.

"That's what I'm talking about on this Labor Day, sitting in his park across the street from the halls of Justice."

"Martin Luther King said that the arc of history is long, but it sways towards justice," Sleepy Willie said.

"How long?" I imitated the Reverend Ralph Abernathy.

"Not long." Willie said, getting into the mood of MLK's cadence.

"How long?" Reverend Abernathy repeated.

"Truth crushed to the ground shall rise again." Reverend King chanted.

"How long?"

"Not long."

"How long?"

Not by the color of their skin . . ."

"How long?"

"Not long."

"How long?"

".. . . But by the content of their character."

"How long."

"Not long."

RECIPES FOR LIFE

"**L**ife," Sleepy Willie said, "is much like a bowl of soup or a bowl of stew. Soups and stews are the stuff of life. A mélange of many things, you just have to know how to mix them for a good balance."

"That sounds like a formula for a stable life," I replied, waiting for Willie to throw the brick.

"I've been thinking about writing a cookbook of soups and stews."

"A cookbook," I replied. "I know you've been cooking for yourself for many years now, living alone as you do. But tell me Willie, do you really think you know enough about cooking to write a book?"

"My life has been a one pot meal, seventy years of soups and stews. Put everything in one pot and there's nothing to it. I can write three cookbooks"

"Besides having a lot of knowledge about cooking, you'll need a special angle to successfully sell a cookbook. Have you been in the cookbook section of any bookstore lately? Man, there are cookbooks that cover every perspective of cooking imaginable."

"Oh, I've got an angle," Willie said.

"Willie, there are cookbooks for vegetarians; gourmet cookbooks, cookbooks on soups, seafood, baking, boiling, broiling, grilling, and stews. Why there was even some guy that came out with a cookbook about cooking meals under your car hood while you're driving. You talk about having an angle. Top that."

"My cookbook will serve people living on a limited budget, who, nevertheless, want to eat well. My cookbook will have recipes for nutritious and hearty meals for people on a pension, social security, low salaries and low spirits. Meals that will feed one person or a small family for a few dollars."

"Such as?" I said showing curiosity.

"Fish head soup," Willie said.

"Fish head soup," I repeated, smiling sarcastically.

"Fish head soup," Willie said resolutely. "I made some yesterday. It came out so good; it brought the idea of a cookbook back to me. Man this soup was demanding to be shared with the world"

"Fish head soup, Willie, that soup sounds repugnant."

"You ain't no Samuel Jackson," Willie said. Only he can say that with meaning. Anyway, I made some fish head soup yesterday that would make you bite your tongue. And, today, after all those flavors finish blending together, it will taste even better than it did last night. Man, it would be too selfish an act to keep this all to myself.

"What?" I said. "I thought I did a pretty good Samuel Jackson. Anyway what goes into fish head soup. Give me the recipe as it would appear in your book."

"Well," Willie said, in a serious tone, "you can use almost any kind of fish heads. Yesterday I went to that fish store across the street from the courthouse. They had some large red snapper heads for sixty-nine cents a pound with some meat still left on them. I had them split the heads in half at the fish store. When I got home I washed them and cleaned them again. Now they were ready for the pot, you see. Then I got all my other ingredients together and put on some music. I don't cook without music. My fish head soup recipe would read like this:

> 3 large snapper heads
> 2 cups water
> 1 cup cut leeks,
> ½ cup celery

1 can chicken broth

2 white potatoes, diced

1 tablespoon bay seasoning

1 large clove crushed garlic

Boil fish heads in water until done, remove bones. Add broth and potatoes, reduce heat. Sauté leeks, garlic, and celery until tender, add to main pot. Add bay seasoning. Salt and pepper to taste. Cover and cook for 30 minutes on low flame.

"Simple," Willie said, quite pleased with himself. It was clear he had given this some thought, or, it might be the acquaintance of time that gave him this self-confidence.

"I must apologize Willie. That doesn't sound as repulsive as it first did. Makes me want to go home with you to taste it. What would a meal like that cost?

"That one would serve four people for less than two dollars a person. But here's the thing, I don't believe in just feeding the flesh, I would also feed the soul. I would suggest that this meal be eaten slow with conversation and the music of Buena Vista Social Club to enjoy the Caribbean ambience of it."

"So you will be dispensing nourishment and enlightenment," I said.

"Recipes for life and living, feeding the body and the soul," Willie said. I will follow each recipe with a few of the sayings of Chairman Willie. This would be a cookbook that treated the whole person."

"The Saying of Chairman Willie," I said. "Whip one on me."

"Men: Never ask a woman about another man," Willie said, "either she will tell you a lie, or something you didn't want to hear. Women: Never ask a man about another woman, either he will tell you a lie, or he will tell you a lie."

"Heavy, heavy. What recipe would that one follow—upside down cake?"

"I don't know. I have yet to lay the whole thing out. But here's one I know will go on a blank page all by itself: Practice self-denial. That would follow my recipe for chicken soup. A soup that would heal your condition, cure your affliction, and bring you to a peaceful place."

"You know Willie, I'm thinking I've heard that phrase the saying of chairman . . . somebody, before. It's coming back. The Saying of Chairman Mao. Yeah, that's where that comes from, Mao Zedong's 'Little Red Book'."

"Soups, Stews and The Sayings of Chairman Willie, that is the title of my book," Willie beamed.

"If I wrote a blurb for your book it would read: Soups, Stews and The Sayings of Chairman Willie, borrowed title/ original recipes."

"Nice try," Willie said, "but no thanks."

"Man I hate to admit it, but you might be on to something here. Over the years you're come up with some of the wildest schemes I've ever heard, this is one I think you should pursue."

"I think I will."

"Give me another recipe with its witticism."

"You know I've had my ups and downs, yes, there have been good times and bad. There was a time when all I could afford was a sack of potatoes. I must have had potato soup for dinner for six months straight. But, you know, if you look for it, something good always occupy the flip side of bad times. You just have to know it's there and find it. Over the years I perfected my potato soup to the point where I eat it even in the good times. I can't think of anything more satisfying on a cold snowy day. The recipe for my potato soup would read like this:

6 medium potatoes

1 cup water

1 can chicken broth

1 can cream of chicken soup

4 slices bacon

1 lb. Smoke sausage

1 clove crush garlic

Peel and cut potatoes into half inch squares. Boil potatoes in water and chicken broth. Add garlic. Cut sausage in bite size pieces and add to pot. Fry bacon. Remove half of the potatoes from pot and purrier in blender. Return potatoes to pot. Add cream of chicken soup stirring well. Cover and cook for 5 minutes. Crumble bacon over soup before serving.

"I would follow that recipe with something I've found to be true in my life: In the end, only the truth shall survive."

"Willie, I'm truly impressed by the fact that you've got this much of this worked out in your head. What you need to do, my man, is write it all out so you can see the entire scope of your project then systemically put it together. Make a list of your recipes and a list of your witticisms to match them up using whatever standard you want to pair them by."

"I'm glad you're finally taking me seriously," Willie said. I think I'm gonna take your advice about writing everything out. I'm gonna let you have a look-see when I'm finish. You want to hear another one of my sayings?"

"Run it."

"I've been working on this one for years now trying to get it just right. I think this is it: The first Africans on the first ship of bondage destine for the Americas, intuitively sensed the need for something to fortify them from the coming centuries of captivity and servitude. So they sent up a wail beseeching God's mercy. God looked down on them and saw that they had nothing. They were naked and in chains. So God, in His wisdom, took the very sound of their lamentation and turned it into their shield and their weapon and today we call that sound music. It is this music in its ever evolving forms that has nourished our people to this day."

"Man, I like that. There is nothing but truth in that statement. From that wail, to the hollows in the fields, to the spirituals, to the blues, to ragtime, to jazz, to rhythm and blues, to hip hop, to now and whatever comes next is where we claim our nourishment. Willie, you know that means even hip hop's got noble roots and virtuous purpose."

"That's the way it is," Willie said. "Hip hop is a descendant of that first wail, though many generations removed."

"Tell me Willie, what would be your favorite recipe in the book?"

"The one I have every New Year," Willie said.

"And what is that?"

"Bring in the New Year Gumbo."

"Bring in the New Year Gumbo," I said. That's a long name for a recipe."

"For the book I'll just call it New Year Gumbo."

"Oh, so you haven't been into the traditional black New Year cuisine?"

"Not for many years now. I love my collard greens and peas and rice, but I've gotten off the heavy pork. Man I done ate my share of chitterlings, hog guts, and pig ears. And I ain't got a bad word for people who still eat like that. You see, I know that change only comes when you see the light."

"William Walker, have you seen the light?" I preached.

"I-have-seen-the-light-brother Ecaroh." Willie said joining in with the spirit of the moment. "I have seen the light and been led out of the darkness."

"I don't know man, a gumbo for New Years?"

"Beats all that grease in them hog guts," Willie said. Plus the soup off the gumbo would be good for a stomach that has had too much alcohol. Here is the recipe for New Year Gumbo:

> 8 cups of water
>
> ½ pound okra
>
> 1 can of tomatoes
>
> 2 crushed garlic cloves
>
> ½ cup of chopped onion
>
> ½ cup of chopped green peppers
>
> ½ cup of chopped celery
>
> 1 can of chicken broth
>
> 1 cup dice potatoes
>
> 1 pound peeled shrimps
>
> ½ pound scallops
>
> 18 clams

1 pound smoked sausage

1 table spoon Cajun seasoning

1 bay leaf

Boil the potatoes in the water with the bay leaf. Add okra and tomatoes. Add Cajun seasoning. Sauté onion, green pepper, garlic, and celery in skillet until tender. Add mixture and chicken broth to pot. Add smoked sausage. Cover and simmer for 30 minutes. Add clams, shrimps, and scallops. Cover and simmer until clams open (3 to 5 Minutes). Happy New Year."

"Willie that sounds really delicious, but it doesn't sound like that is a cheap meal to make."

"An enlightened pygmy towers like a giant over the average size narrow-minded person," Willie said. "Even financially scrapped people should eat a relatively expensive meal once in a while."

"Is that the Sleepy Willie saying to go with your New Year gumbo?"

"No. The saying to go after the gumbo is: While you were waiting, get up and go—done got up and gone."

"Kind of a slogan for procrastinators," I said.

"Exactly," Willie said. "And that's what I'm gonna do right now so I can get home to work on my book. Get up and go done got up and gone."

TAKE ME TO THE WATER

Sleepy Willie hasn't been in the Two Cousin Bar for two weeks. I called him on the phone a few times, but he wasn't home. So I decided I'd better check on him. I went to the bar first. Willie wasn't there and no one there had seen him this evening. I walked four blocks up the Grand Concourse to Willie's apartment building hoping I would find him home. I rang the buzzer to his apartment and the door was buzzed opened. I took the elevator to the third floor and knocked on 3f. I could hear music coming through the door, but I couldn't make out clearly what was playing. Soon I heard footsteps coming to the door. Then I saw the peephole open and shut. The door opened. The music came clear. It was Nina Simone singing 'Take me to the Water,' an old gospel song about baptism.

"What you know, Ecaroh," Willie said cheerfully as he opened the door, "come on in man."

"Willie, I just dropped by to check on you," I said as we walked back to the living room. You haven't been to the bar in a good while and when I called you didn't answer, so I got a little worried. What's up buddy? How are you?"

"I'm doing pretty well," Willie said, as we took seats, "just been very busy. I was going to get in touch with you in the morning, because there is something I want to invite you and your family to."

My mind focused on Nina singing slowly "Take . . . me . . . to . . . the . . . water. Take . . . me . . . to . . . the . . . water. Take . . . me . . . to . . . the . . . water."

"I want you to come to church Sunday," Sleepy Willie said.
"What?" I answered.

" I want you to come to church this Sunday coming."

"Willie don't tell me Mrs. Brentwood's got you recruiting church goers."

"No, it's nothing like that," Willie said. "You see, I've joined the church and this Sunday I'm going to be baptized. I want you to be there to witness my acceptance of Jesus Christ as my Lord and Savior."

"Take . . . me . . . to . . . the . . . water. Take . . . me . . . to . . . the . . . water. Take . . . me . . . to . . . the . . . water." Nina sang.

"You joined the . . . you're going to be . . . you want me to . . . Mrs. Brentwood what have you done to Willie," I said, somewhat rhetorically. "So this is why you haven't been to the bar lately. You've been going to church. When did you join?" I asked.

"Yeah, I was thinking it would be best if I stayed away from the bar while I get this thing together. Then last Sunday I was sitting next to Mrs. Brentwood at church. The preacher asked for anyone who was empty of heart to come forward and the sound from the choir filled my very soul. The only way I can explain it is that a spirit plucked me from my seat, before I knew what had happened I found myself standing in front of the preacher, ready. So I made the public commitment last Sunday."

"Willie, I'm very happy for you. That you have found redemption," I said pretentiously.

"I can tell that you don't mean it."

I didn't say anything in response. I was being insincere and I needed a moment or two to ponder why. Sleepy Willie is the best friend I ever had. He would do anything for my family or me. We are very fond of each other. Now he's found Mrs. Brentwood and she's made him happy. Then he went to the church and that's making him happy. Now he's seeking God and the ultimate happiness. I should be happy for him. I've got a wife and family to make my life full. Willie deserves whatever makes his life more complete.

"No man, I'm sorry," I said. "I think I was just so surprised my mind wasn't clear. What time man, what time?"

"What time?"

"Yeah, what time is the baptism?"

"The baptism will be after regular service, but you should come for the full service and that starts at eleven o'clock." Willie said.

"Man I don't know what to say."

"You don't have say anything," Willie said. It's been a long time in the coming. Too long a time. I don't want to sound like I'm preaching, but I hope that it won't take you as long to find your way to a church. I know your wife goes to church and she takes your children with her. Ecaroh, for the first time in my life, I don't want to give any advice, but it may be time for you to find your way to some church, somewhere. And I just want to tell you that."

"I appreciate it Willie. I imagine you've got everything under control for the baptism, but if there is anything I can do?"

"No. Nothing. Just be there Sunday. I bought a new blue suit, a shirt and tie and some new shoes, although I won't be wearing them during the main event. We're having a special little celebration dinner at Mrs. Brentwood's apartment after the baptism. A few friends from the church will be there and I'd like it if you'd come and bring your family."

"You can count on it buddy. What time? Can we bring something?"

"Say, about three o'clock," Willie said. "What about a cake."

"Willie, we've been friends for a long time and although I feel like I'm losing you and our way of life, I'm honor bound to give you my complete support."

"What do you mean?" Willie said, showing his annoyance. Oh, now I see what you're getting at. Ecaroh, you need a beer man."

"Yeah, if you got some."

Willie went to the kitchen and returned with one beer. "There is more in the refrigerator," he said as he sat down. Look Ecaroh, inside I'm the same person you been talking to all these years. My opinions and outlook are the same. I think I'm a pretty decent person, always have been. I've done some things in my life that I'm not proud of, for the most part I'm me and through it all God has remain my friend. I've always been a believer but now I've found a church home with people I enjoy worshiping with. You're still the best buddy I've got. We'll still meet at the Two Cousins Bar and talk part of the night away. Only the Two Cousins are going to have to buy a coffee machine. All these nightly meetings I'm been attending at the church has given me a liking for coffee."

"Coffee machine?" I smirked.

"Oh, I'll still have a beer, and an occasional brandy which you can buy," Willie said trying to create our usual financial dispute and some normalcy in the discussion."

"You'll have to buy your own beer and brandy," I joined Willie in the plot. "I'll buy the coffee."

"So all is good then," Willie said. I can expect to see you at the church Sunday, and at the dinner later . . . right?"

"All set," I said finishing my beer. I handed the can to Willie as I rose from the couch. Willie walked me to the door and we said goodnight with an embrace. I don't know what brought the thought in my head except that it was all in the atmosphere, all entwined in the changes in Willie's life, it was all over the place. And as I waited for the elevator the thought came: the next thing Willie is going to tell me is that he is getting married. The elevator arrived; I got in and pressed the ground floor button.